E IS FOR EXOTIC

Also by Alison Tyler

———

Best Bondage Erotica

Best Bondage Erotica 2

Exposed

The Happy Birthday Book of Erotica

Heat Wave: Sizzling Sex Stories

Luscious: Stories of Anal Eroticism

The Merry XXXmas Book of Erotica

Red Hot Erotica

Slave to Love

Three-Way

Caught Looking (with Rachel Kramer Bussel)

A Is for Amour

B Is for Bondage

C Is for Coeds

D Is for Dress-Up

F Is for Fetish

G Is for Games

H Is for Hardcore

E IS FOR EXOTIC

IS FOR EXOTIC

EROTIC STORIES
EDITED BY ALISON TYLER

CLEIS
PRESS

Published in the United States by Cleis Press Inc., P.O. Box 14697, San Francisco, California 94114.

Printed in the United States.
Cover design: Scott Idleman
Text design: Karen Quigg
Cleis Press logo art: Juana Alicia
First Edition.
10 9 8 7 6 5 4 3 2 1

ACKnowLEDGments

Extraordinary Exaltations go to:

Krista Barragar

Violet Blue

Frédérique Delacoste

Diane Levinson

Felice Newman

Barbara Pizio

The Lust Bites Ladies

and SAM, always.

If you don't know where you are going, any road will get you there.
—LEWIS CARROLL

It is good to have an end to journey towards; but it is the journey that matters in the end.
—URSULA K. LE GUIN

contents

ix   Introduction: Everybody Knows

1   Spider • DONNA GEORGE STOREY

15   Native Tongue • SHANNA GERMAIN

25   The Moments • MICHAEL HEMMINGSON

35   Line Shack • RAKELLE VALENCIA

43   Bus Ride • KIS LEE

53   Wet • MATHILDE MADDEN

63   Heat • T. C. CALLIGARI

73   Arizona, Ireland, New England • CHEYENNE BLUE

79   The Things That Go On at Siesta Time • SASKIA WALKER

91   Mad Dogs • LISABET SARAI

105   Learning His Ropes • TERESA NOELLE ROBERTS

115   Essence • NIKKI MAGENNIS

123   Un, Deux, Trois • ALISON TYLER

137   About the Editor

INTRODUCTION:
EVERYBODY KNOWS

E VERYBODY KNOWS…

Everybody knows that exotic locations lend themselves to erotic explorations. How could it be any other way? The crisp hotel sheets, or white-hot sand, or chilled tropical drinks—*these* are the perfect ingredients for a combustible foreign romance. But what makes a location exotic? Must a pair of lovers be strolling along the silvery Seine in order for their kiss to be extreme? Or does bondage sex on a tour bus to Vegas count?

According to the talented thirteen authors in this collection, exotic connections can occur anywhere. On a crowded train in Mexico City, as in "Heat" by T. C. Calligari:

Slowly, as the train trundled along, the hand wedged firmer between her folds, one finger moving forward and back, flicking over her clit. Erica's knees would have buckled had she not been wedged between so many people.

The lights flickered off on the train and her mystery man took that moment to push two fingers up into her cunt. Erica moaned, her eyes closed. But the stranger's hand never stopped its slow movement within her.

Or after a scare from a "Spider" in Tokyo, as in Donna George Storey's erotic tale:

"Do you know shibari?" he asked with the familiar gleam in his eye.

"Is that like those porn pictures where they tie women up so they look like they're caught in a spider's web?" I replied, hoping my saucy tone would hide the fact my pulse was racing.

"I forgot that you're scared of spiders. You shouldn't be. They bring good luck."

I laughed uncomfortably. "I'm not so sure about that."

He lifted his eyebrows. "Let me teach you."

Or on a deserted ranch, as seen in Rakelle Valencia's "Line Shack":

Wave after wave of her orgasm gripped and sucked at him. Her legs wrapped around him to hold him more tightly into her. That was his undoing. That last slam, powered by the force of muscular, feminine thighs brought him to his limits. It felt like a glorious eternity, but it had only been mere minutes that they stayed locked with each other. Flint adjusted himself, then zipped up, reaching next to help his wife with her clothes and boots.

"Best get the mule loaded if we're to make the line shack before nightfall."

Or even in a muddy field on the way home after a miserable rain-drenched camping trip, as in Mathilde Madden's super-sexy story, "Wet":

The tree branches are still dripping, even though the rain has stopped. Water splashes down on my face. It's probably wetter here, under the tree, than outside in the lane now. Wetter still now Michael is on top of me, kissing his way down my muddy half-dressed body. I look at him. He's filthy, too.

Muddier than he ever got on our wet weekend of camping. He looks like he'll never be clean again. I kind of like that.

So prepare yourself for an exotic journey, if not always to faraway lands, then to faraway fantasies.

No passport required.

XXX,
Alison Tyler

DONNA GEORGE STOREY

SPIDER

SCAPE. THAT'S WHY I LEFT TOKYO, to get away from trouble— thrilling, addictive, going-nowhere sex with a married guy. I lined up a few English teaching jobs in Kyoto, rented a studio in a "mansion" apartment building in the western district, and planned to spend my free time contemplating life's transience at picturesque temples. No more desperate quickies in public restrooms, no more butt fucking in hot spring baths after midnight, no more blow jobs in a private compartment in the Shinkansen. Unfortunately, I forgot to add "no letting gorgeous neighbors tie me up and screw my brains out" to the list, but I didn't think of that until I was already in a bind again.

Oddly enough, my fall from virtue started when I went outside to do my laundry. The cold-water hookup for the washing machine was located next to my front door, and I always began by hosing off the week's accumulation of dust from the lid. That's what I was doing when I first met Ito.

Actually, what I was really doing when I met Ito was screaming my head off in terror. Because when I sprayed away some cottony cobwebs behind the washer, I suddenly made the acquaintance of a new neighbor I was none too happy to see—a very large spider. A fucking huge spider, as large as my outstretched hand, its hairy legs as fat as fingers.

I screamed and jumped about three feet in the air, screamed again and aimed the hose, my only weapon handy, directly at the spider's swollen brown body. This turned out to be a mistake, because the creature rocketed about six feet across the pathway and vanished in the weeds. No doubt it was already plotting a counterattack. And it knew just where to find me.

I was still whimpering when I heard a deep voice drifting down from the balcony above.

"*Dô shitan desu ka?*" What's the matter?

I looked up and saw a slim male figure leaning against the railing, cigarette in his hand. His name was Ito, although I wouldn't learn that for a few days, and I wouldn't call him by his first name, Toshima, until we'd already had several rounds of very hot sex. But at that moment, my heart pounding, my breath coming fast, I silently called him the most gorgeous hunk of eye candy I'd seen in some time.

"It was a spider," I replied in quivering Japanese. "Really big. This big." I held out my hand, the fingers clawed in a spidery pose.

Ito arched an eyebrow. "A spider?"

"A very scary spider." A *tarantula* was more like it, but I didn't have my dictionary handy to check for the Japanese word.

I admit part of me hoped he'd come down and help me out. It wouldn't have been the first time my beseeching blue eyes had lured an attractive Japanese man to my side. But Ito just gave me a cool smile. Far from offering to help a maiden in distress, he seemed to take genuine pleasure in watching me squirm.

For the next few days, I made a habit of peeking behind the washing machine before I went inside my apartment. I searched my room, too, my body tensed as I scanned every corner and crevice for a sign of that hideous, eight-legged monster. More than once I woke up to a tickling sensation moving over my chest, but since I never found any real spiders in my bed, I convinced myself that bit of trouble was gone for good.

I did see Ito again, though, by the mailboxes after my Wednesday night English class at Hitachi. I assumed from the salaryman's suit and tie that he was coming home from work. He looked tired and older than he had in his Sunday morning jeans—on our first meeting he'd struck me more like an insolent college student than an office worker drone—but when he saw me, a mischievous light switched on his dark eyes.

"See anything scary lately?" he asked.

"Not until now." My Japanese was good enough for flirting when I wasn't frightened out of my wits.

He grinned. And invited me out for fried noodles at the grill near the subway station.

I was tempted to say no. After all, he'd laughed at me in my moment of need. But somehow I couldn't refuse him then, or the time after that when he asked me to join him at a *karaoké* box with some friends, or when he invited me to dinner at a Chinese place near Kawaramachi Sanjo. Yes, the attraction was physical. It was hard to resist those swooping, velvet eyes and the lush black hair. His shapely ass and muscular arms called out for some tactile exploration as well, and after a beer or two, I even came to see the charm of that mocking smile.

But Ito did one thing that turned me on more than any of the other guys I'd dated here. He would only speak to me in Japanese. I was used to being the honorable English *sensei*, even in bed, but now I was the one to flounder for the right word while he watched calmly, always the expert, always in control. He even corrected my mistakes—none too gently at times—but I found I enjoyed this linguistic domination, or at least my body did. After an evening struggling through a conversation with Ito, my panties were so wet, I was sure he could smell me.

I was definitely ready to skip the Zen meditation for a little Sumo wrestling on my futon, but even after our third date, Ito merely gave me a curt bow of good night and headed up the stairs to his place. That left me to go home alone, change my damp underwear, and lounge in front of Sony Music TV while I tried to decide whether to masturbate or just fall asleep hungry.

Then came the knock at the door. Deliverymen and proselytizing Mormons usually kept to the daylight hours, and I wasn't expecting any visitors. Still, I dutifully went to the intercom and asked in my most polite Japanese who it was.

"*Boku da yo. Ito.*"

So much for the new pair of dry panties. Just the sound of that low, gruff voice had me gushing. I quickly pulled my cotton bathrobe over my nightshirt and opened the door.

"I forgot something," he said. "May I come in?"

He'd never set foot in my apartment—what could he have forgotten?

— 4 —

I didn't have to wonder for long. In two steps, Ito pushed me up against the wall of the entryway. I was surprised at the power of his lean body. I was trapped, enveloped, his arms and legs wrapped all around me as if he had more than one pair of each. Our gazes locked. His eyes glittered in the shadows, and I would have been trembling if I hadn't been too stunned to move.

But Ito was moving now, his fingers soft and teasing. First he touched my cheek, an oddly tender gesture that sent electric jolts straight to my pussy. His hand slid over my neck and shoulder, snaking under the collar of the robe, pinching my nipple through my shirt. Wherever he touched me, the skin grew warm and slick, as if he were wrapping my flesh in bands of hot, wet silk. His other hand slipped through the robe from below, cupping my ass, probing the crack gently.

I let out a soft moan.

He smiled and wiggled a finger under the elastic of my panties to stroke my swollen pussy lips. I caught my breath as he found my clit. Ito had left the door half open—just the sort of edgy sex game I'd vowed to give up—yet the more he strummed, the more I liked the idea of doing it right there against the wall of my *genkan* for all of Kyoto to see.

"Do you always get this wet so fast?" he asked, holding up a glistening finger.

Before I could argue it was all his fault, he started painting my lips with my own juices, squinting in concentration as if he were applying real makeup, a bright red geisha's pout. Only then did he lean forward and kiss me, our first kiss, tasting of Chinese spices, beer and my own desire.

He pulled away first. "I could tell you needed this all evening. Please accept my apologies for not helping sooner. Until next time, *ne*?" he said and left without even bothering to close the door behind him.

I wasn't sure whether to curse him or laugh, but at least he had settled my plans for the rest of the evening. Masturbate it would be. I stumbled back into the room, rolled onto my futon and hiked my nightshirt up under my arms. Ito was right. I was very wet. My whole body was covered with a thin film of sweat, and my hands skidded over my breasts, palming the nipples, flicking them with my thumbs, sliding farther down to rub my swollen clit. The faint click-clicking sound of aroused pussy filled my ears, and I couldn't resist licking the sticky juice, slowly and submissively, as if I were sucking his fingers instead of my own. Suddenly, my hands did seem thicker and stronger, gliding over my body with a will of their own, not so much to pleasure me, but to remind me that I'd been wrapped up like a package in invisible bonds that pressed gently into my skin, softening me for the feast to come.

Mataserareta. "You kept me waiting in frustration." Just saying the word is torture enough, but when you live in Japan, you come to learn how waiting weaves its way into the fabric of life to the point that they really do need a special word for it. I was used to waiting for Yoshida, that's par for the course when you're boning a married guy, but Ito was a free man, or so he told me. Yet for almost a week after our very promising encounter in my entryway, he simply disappeared.

The wait was definitely frustrating, but I had a feeling he'd be back for more.

I was right.

I'd just returned from my evening class in Otsu, and even before I put my key in the lock, I sensed a presence inside. Heart pounding, I cracked the door and peeked into the dark room. Dark that is except for the glowing tip of a cigarette and a male silhouette outlined against the city lights that glittered through the window beyond.

I snapped on the light. Ito regarded me calmly from my futon, which I left lying open "thousand year style" like the careless housekeeper I was.

"You scared me." My pulse was still racing, but for a different reason now.

"You look pretty when you're scared." He made the Japanese "come here" gesture that looks oddly like an American good-bye.

The proper response, of course, would have been a few choice observations like "You have some fucking nerve ignoring me for a week, then breaking into my apartment like a pervert." But I wasn't quite sure how to say "fucking nerve" in Japanese and my dictionary was buried at the bottom of my book bag. Besides, I was curious to see what his next move would be.

Docile as any well-bred Japanese miss, I sat down beside him. The mattress was warm and I wondered how long he'd been lurking here.

Ito ran his hand down my back, a businesslike gesture. "Is this shirt important to you? Expensive?"

"Not particularly, it's just something I wear for work." I frowned, not quite following the turn of conversation.

He nodded and reached toward the low table next to the bed. I noticed a bottle of *saké* sitting next to one of my Japanese teacups. Ito dipped his fingers in the cup and anointed each breast with a few drops of the chilled liquid. My nipples immediately tightened into points. Farther down, the secret muscles in my belly clenched in sympathy, as if Ito's cold fingers had crept up under my skirt, too.

"Hey, stop, you're going to ruin it," I protested.

A smile playing over his lips, Ito took part of the collar in each hand and pulled. Hard.

I cried out at the sound of tearing cloth, buttons flying.

"I think I already have ruined it. Sorry."

"Fuck you," I shot back in English.

In spite of his claim that his English was poor, Ito seemed to understand perfectly. "Sure, if that's what you want."

Of course, I did.

Lying beneath him, my legs trapped between his, his hard cock pressing against me through his jeans, the fate of one boring white blouse didn't seem so important after all.

But there was still more waiting to endure. Ito stroked and sucked my breasts for what seemed like hours until I was whimpering and arching up against him, the heat of my longing forced inward until my whole body melted, soaking the sheet beneath me with sweat and pussy juice. At last, he moved lower, wrapping his arm under my thighs to hold my legs together while he flicked my clit with the tip of his tongue. I instinctively tried to open my legs, but Ito tightened his hold.

"Don't move. Don't make a sound," he whispered.

I bit back a groan. It wasn't so easy to be still or quiet with that magic tongue sending sizzling jolts of pleasure up my spine. In fact, I suspected I was about to be doing some serious moaning and thrashing very soon.

"Is it okay if I come?" I bleated out.

Ito looked up at me, his lips and chin glistening. "That was a mistake."

I thought I'd used the right words—in Japanese you say "go" instead of "come"—but I wasn't exactly focused on proper grammar. "Did I say it wrong?"

"The problem is you shouldn't have asked at all," Ito said with a tight smile. He sat up and lit another cigarette.

I knew we weren't talking Japanese Culture, because my married lover always liked a warning so he could slip inside in time for the grand finale. Ito was making up his own rules, but I was too horny to submit so easily this time. Besides, he owed me something for that shirt.

I crawled over to him and rested my hand on the obvious tent pole in his jeans. "If I promise to be good now, will you fuck me?"

He stared down at me with narrowed eyes.

"I'll do anything you want," I added.

Ito took a long drag on his cigarette. "All right. Get me the belt of your bathrobe. I'll need those stockings you're wearing and something else—a scarf or another pair of stockings will do."

With my wrists bound over my head and my thighs and ankles lashed together with the panty hose, I was more at his mercy than ever, but I did get a front row seat for a strip show that didn't disappoint. Ito was even tastier naked, with sculpted shoulders; a smooth, golden chest; and an uncut cock jutting out, all hard and ready. If I hadn't been tied up, I couldn't have resisted wrapping my hand around him, licking the swollen head, and taking him deep into my mouth. As I lay there, drooling, it occurred to me oral sex might be all we could manage anyway. How could he fuck me with my legs tied so tightly together?

Ito, on the other hand, had no doubts. He fished a condom from his pocket, straddled me, and pushed his cock down between my thighs. Shifting his hips a bit to get the right position, he slid right inside.

The constriction was definitely a plus. His shaft pressed up against my clit and my cunt was so compressed and swollen, I could feel the knob of his cock stretching me as he thrust in and out through my tingling hole. Ito was a real Mr. Octopus, bending to suckle one breast, twisting the other nipple between his fingers. In no time at all, the orgasm he'd chased away came creeping back, a coil of heat glowing and growing in my belly. I wasn't going to ask permission this time. I squeezed my eyes shut and swallowed down my cries as my pleasure exploded, making me strain against the bonds, shooting up through my chest to blow my skull open as wide and black as the midnight sky.

Afterward we lay twined together, the discarded panty hose, belt, and my ripped blouse piled around us.

"I thought you'd forgotten me," I confessed, an easy thing to do now that he was curled around me, his smile much sweeter in his post-come gratitude.

"That's another mistake," he said lazily, stroking my hair. "I think about you all the time. It was hard for me to wait, but I know surprises excite you. And that excites me."

I couldn't help smiling, secretly, into his shoulder.

He was as caught up in this as I was.

Two days later Ito showed up at my door with a gift tied up in a traditional wrapping cloth.

I smiled until I saw what was inside: a coil of golden rope, with the sweet fragrance of new-mown hay. "Thanks, but what do I do with it?"

"Do you know *shibari*?" he asked with the familiar gleam in his eye.

"Is that like those porn pictures where they tie women up so they look like they're caught in a spider's web?" I replied, hoping my saucy tone would hide the fact my pulse was racing.

"I forgot that you're scared of spiders. You shouldn't be. They bring good luck."

"That thing wasn't a spider, it was a tarantula." Since our first meeting, I'd looked up the Japanese name—*jorōgumo*—the prostitute spider, a word that suddenly seemed prophetic.

"Big spiders bring more luck."

I laughed uncomfortably. "I'm not so sure about that."

He lifted his eyebrows. "Let me teach you."

I hesitated. If I really meant to get away from kinky sex, now was the time to draw the line. I couldn't deny, however, that Ito was a good teacher. My Japanese had already improved a lot, and I was curious what else he could teach me about ropes, and worlds where the rules were different, and maybe even big, scary spiders.

Besides, I was so turned on by the idea of him tying me up, I was already creaming in my pants.

And so, just as he commanded, I peeled my clothes off and sat on the futon, my back straight, my legs folded under me in proper Japanese style. With a nod of approval, Ito wrapped the doubled rope around my waist and then pulled the loose ends through the loop to make a belt.

"Lie back and bring your knees to your chest."

As if in a dream, I watched him wrap the rope around my bent leg several times, binding my thigh to my shin. Next he tied it crosswise underneath my bent knee. The bonds were softer than I expected and made a surprisingly pretty picture, too, layers of golden rope crisscrossing over my pale skin.

"Give me your hand."

I reached toward him, my arm trembling faintly in anticipation. He circled more rope around my wrist and secured it to my knee. My right leg and wrist received the same careful treatment, so that in the end I was lying flat on my back, legs spread wide in a fuck-me position. Ito was obviously enjoying this view. Under the heat of his steady gaze, I felt my pussy lips swelling and blushing deep red, and then, to my embarrassment, came a gush of hot juices, trickling down my slit, pooling under my ass.

Ito brushed a finger gently along the slick cleft. "It's better if you close your eyes. Spiders might look ugly, but they feel nice."

I swallowed hard. What had I gotten myself into? But at this point I was literally in no position to refuse. I closed my eyes.

For a moment, there was nothing, just the cool air on my exposed flesh, but then I felt a feathery sensation creeping slowly from the edge of the rope down my thigh. Of course it was just his fingers—a joke— but then the image of the spider's thick brown legs flashed against my eyelids. My stomach tightened. I realized I'd been holding my breath.

The fingers moved lower, teasing the crack of my ass. I'd let lovers touch me there before, but they'd always been quick to put something inside—a finger, a cock. Ito's hand hovered, soft and achingly slow, his fingers tapping and dancing over the moist, exquisitely sensitive skin.

I squirmed instinctively, like a little dog happy to please her master, begging for more.

"Have you changed your mind about spiders yet?"

I moaned, the best answer my lips could manage.

As before, the punishment was swift. In the next moment the spider—and the delicious sensation—was gone.

"I do like it. Oh, please, do it again." If he wanted me to beg, I'd do it. I'd do anything to have those fingers back.

"No, I think the spider's hungry now."

I tensed, imagining a bite, but instead I felt a pillowy softness pressing against my asshole. Not fingers this time, it was lips, kissing me gently in that forbidden place. I almost giggled—did spiders kiss ass?—but then came the hot tongue, rolling over my crack like molten silk, darting French-style into the small, lipless mouth. The laugh faded into a sigh. I could feel that tingling heat in my toes, my teeth, my clit. My whole body was dissolving into syrup. In that tiny corner of my brain still capable of thought, I remembered that this is exactly what spiders do—reduce their prey's body to a soup then suck up the sweet juices, leaving only the shell behind.

Maybe it wouldn't be such a bad way to go after all.

It got even better. The spider fingers returned, crawling lightly across my belly, over the mossy hill of my mons to my clit.

"That's really good. Spiders feel nice," I babbled, my limbs twitching helplessly in Ito's golden web. Caught between the tickling fingers and the lapping tongue, I had nowhere to go but up, leaping, twirling, spinning as I climaxed in quivering spasms. My moans were so loud, I'm sure I disturbed a few neighbors this time around, too.

When I opened my eyes, Ito was smiling down at me, just like he had the first day I saw him. He leaned over and touched his lips to mine. Now it was my turn to feast on him, his saliva mixed with a new, faintly earthy flavor.

Yes, I moved to Kyoto to get away from crazy sex. This meant, I imagined, a life of celibacy or at best a tepid rebound relationship: lights out, missionary position only. Fortunately, Ito was waiting here to remind me that if you're open to new things, life in a foreign land can be full of surprises. And some of those surprises are very nice indeed.

Besides, thanks to him, I did see spiders differently after that night. They still got my pulse racing—especially the big ones—but I never tried to harm them again. I'd smile and watch them scuttle to safety, remembering how luck comes in the strangest guises.

NATIVE TONGUE

VERYTHING ON THE MENU is foreign to me. The waiter, who's wearing a blue T-shirt with a bunch of words on it that I don't know or want to know, waits for me to order. The menu has a few words I know, too many for my liking—*ceviche* and *coca light* and *burrito*—but I skip those, pretend I haven't seen them, and point only to the ones I don't know.

When the waiter leaves, I look out over the ocean and listen to the other diners talking in a language I don't know. Their conversation washes past my ears, no different than ocean waves. There's only one other white person in the place, and his Spanish carries the same musical roll and lilt as the words of those sitting at the table with him.

I love being in a place where I have no language. Sitting here at this open-air restaurant, waiting for Margret and not understanding a damn word, it's heaven. There was a time when I thought I wanted to know every language in the world. That's why I started working as a translator eight years ago. But now, I wish I could take that desire back. That's the funny thing about languages: like learning to read, you can't take it back. Once you know a word it can never become a mystery again.

Believe it or not, with all the languages I know, I don't know Spanish. When you translate for a living Spanish is the least requested, because everyone knows it, so I never bothered to learn. And that's allegedly why I've come to the least tourist-ridden beach in Costa Rica, to immerse myself in the Spanish language for three weeks.

But in truth, I have come to meet my lover. Margret's plane landed at noon, and barring unexpected delays or bad roads, she should arrive just in time to join me in the feast of whatever it is I just ordered. I'm dressed in a bikini—black, to match my hair that I'm wearing in one long braid down my back—and a black and red sarong that's wrapped around me like a strapless dress. It's a sarong that Margret bought me last time I saw her, and I could tell from the light in her eyes that she liked the way I looked in it.

The waiter sets down the beers I asked for—that was one thing I knew how to say. Brand names are surprisingly and sadly universal.

He gestures to the empty seat with a flat palm. I don't know if he's questioning where the other half of my party is or if he's asking if he can join me.

"Soon," I say, and I'm struck by my own desire to communicate even as I'm trying to leave all communication behind.

When he leaves, I sip my beer and lean back in my chair with a sigh. I'm jet-lagged, but only a little, and the peace that the beer and the breeze and the lack of conscious understanding bring is amazing. I watch the ocean break across the sand. Out near the water, a woman in a swimsuit races the waves. She is the color of dark honey, tanned and toned against her off-white bikini. I am lost in pictures. I will my brain to shut off, to stop finding words for every color and movement and object.

My bottle of beer is nearly gone before I feel hands tugging at my braid. The hands climb up the back of my head, and then down over my eyes. I bring my own hand up to feel Margret's thin wrist, layered over with tiny metal bracelets. They jangle when she tugs on my ear. And then she is slipping her arms around me, nearly choking me, to hug me from behind. She doesn't care who sees, and wrapped in her car-cooled arms and her turpentine and lavender scent, I don't either.

Margret lets me out of her backward bear hug and sits across from me. She is long-limbed and reedy, with big blue eyes and shoulder-length curls the ruddy tint of cedar shavings. She grins at me, showing the little space between her front teeth that I love, and then tips the top of her beer bottle toward me. We clink bottles, and then drink.

"Margret," I say.

It is the only word, other than my own name, that can pass between us. Margret speaks only her native Dutch. Nothing else. That's how we met earlier this year. She needed an interpreter in the States when her artwork was showing around town. Because she lived in Italy, I assumed she spoke Italian or French or even a bit of English. But no. As it turned out, she'd lived all over the world, but only spoke Dutch. A dying language, and one I didn't speak a word of.

Still, she was gorgeous. And her paintings were the same—landscapes so infused with emotion and light that you forgot they were just paintings of trees and clouds. She didn't seem to think in words, only images.

I found her another translator from our company, but not before I'd fallen for her. Hard. It wasn't just her curls or that gap-toothed smile. It was the language, or lack of it.

My partner, Helen, is a dictionary writer. Woman of all words, always the right word. In our house, every word has meaning; every word has weight, has to be picked over and examined, dead or alive, until it can be stored and measured and accounted for. "Good night," is never just good night. It might be "Good night, I hate you," or "Good night, why won't you feed the cat?" or "Good night, let's fuck." But it is never, ever just good night.

Helen will say things like, "Did you know there is no word in the English language that is commonly used to describe a woman's private parts?" even as I have my tongue or fingers in her private parts. Even as I bring those private parts to places that have words: *wet* and *shudder* and *moan* and *orgasm*.

With Margret, there is no good night. There are no private parts. Well, there are private parts, but there is no worry over what to call them. There is just the way she puts her fingers to her nether lips and parts them for me. The way I dip my fingers in her as though she is the ocean. And there is the way she's looking at me right now, blue eyes narrowed, her soft bare foot beneath the table, wrapped around the back of my calf.

The waiter brings us plates of food: some kind of fish with crackers, little crab legs and calamari-like rings in a red sauce. When he has filled our table and pointed at our beers and we nod yes, Margret lets her hand rest on his arm for a brief second before he turns away. She says something in Dutch.

I shake my head, but I can't hide my smile, or the way her words made my insides feel. Only Margret would say something to a Costa-Rican waiter in Dutch and expect him to understand.

After we stuff ourselves silly, feeding each other bits of seafood and slices of fruit, we go down to the beach. Margret shimmies out of her sundress, and for a few seconds, I open my mouth to tell her it's not a nude beach. Which is a silly instinct, considering. And it doesn't matter anyway, because she's wearing a tiny bikini under the dress. Dark blue, only slightly darker than the ocean and the same color as her eyes. It covers her small round breasts in two triangles. Her nipples point in the triangles' direct centers. I want to drag my tongue across the fabric like a cat.

She takes my hand and tugs me toward the ocean. I drop my sarong to the ground on the way. We walk through the waves to the point where the water evens out. It is nearly up to our chins, but so calm that we can touch the sand at the bottom on our tiptoes and don't get knocked over.

Her sigh as she leans back into the warm water is one I recognize. It's a sigh of pleasure. I join her as we lean back and float, our faces to the sky. There is no sound but the surf and, far off, the chatter of birds or people. It is hard to tell which is which, and so I tell myself they are birds.

Floating like this, I wonder at how this can be, so many ways to love, and I'm thankful there are no words to describe this kind of love or that one. It isn't as though I don't love Helen. I do. It's just that there are too many words now. In the beginning, the words were stones we dropped into the water to walk on, to go to the same places together.

Now the words are stones that we carry in our fists, our arms always drawn back, ready to fling.

Margret's hand finds mine beneath the water, and I curl my fingers over hers. Already our skin is salt-sucked and wrinkled. Even so, I swear she's the softest thing I've ever felt. I slide my hand up her arm, pull her closer to me. She laughs, and grabs my belly. The water pushes us closer, pulls us apart, and still, her lips find mine. Her silent tongue enters my mouth, touches all the places where we make words and soothes them as easily as the sea.

When we are sandy and salty and wet as we can handle, we stand under the simple outdoor shower until the cold water makes us shiver. Then I lead Margret on the path up from the beach. Soon, we're at the edge of the rainforest. They're that close to each other, forest and beach and ocean, as though they're siblings, sisters that couldn't bear to live together, but couldn't bear to be too far apart.

Beneath the canopy of trees, we follow the path up and up. The sunlight makes stained-glass patterns as it passes through the leaves and vines and lands at our feet. Small brown and white monkeys swing from tree to tree above our heads, making *oo-oo* noises as they go. Margret reaches back and takes my hand and we walk like that, our footsteps crackling twigs, our breath puffing without sound.

Tucked back in the woods, the hut I rented for us is just that—a hut. Open to the air around the top, with a plain hammock on the front porch. Inside, there is only the bed, and a tiny table. Margret doesn't seem to care. She runs and throws herself on the bed so that the mattress shoots her back up in the air, sends her damp curls flying out in all directions around her. She pats the blanket next to her. Come, no matter what language you don't speak.

I start to lie down next to her on the bed, but she shakes her head. She makes a shimmying motion, her hips moving back and forth across the simple blanket. I tuck my thumbs into the sides of my bikini bottom, wiggling my hips. Like this?

She puts her hands to her lips and nods. I slide my bikini bottom down, half inch by half inch, shaking my body with it. Compared to Margret, I'm curvy. My belly slides in above my round hips, accentuates the curvy ass that I can only keep in shape with daily bike rides. She seems to delight in my curves as much as I delight in her angularity.

There is no "Am I skinny enough?" or "Are you sure you should be eating that?" There is only me, sliding my bikini bottom down over the wet and salty curves of me. There is only Margret watching from the bed, her lips parted, her own damp body soaking into the blanket.

I slide the bottom down all the way, step out of it. Margret runs her tongue across her bottom lip and waits. I unhook the back of my bikini top. There isn't as much here to shimmy out of, so I just let it fall away. I've had my nipples pierced since I last saw her: two tiny blue stones hanging from each peak. Tiny blue stones that match her eyes.

Her eyes get big when she sees them, and she puts her hand over her mouth. Then she rolls over on all fours and crawls across the bed toward me. She takes my hand and pulls me down, until I'm kneeling on the bed. When she leans forward, the smell of saltwater is everywhere. Then her tongue is on my nipple, round and round the nipple and the jewelry. Her warm mouth sucks. The piercings are newly healed, sensitive, but in a good way. Margret catches one between her teeth, and pulls up. My body reacts like she's pulling on a string tied to my belly, the inside of my thighs. Everything pulls up with her mouth.

"Margret," I breathe. She smiles at her name, and then runs her mouth lower, down the flat expanse of my belly. When she hits my thighs, she rolls on her back and scoots herself under me. She uses her tongue to paint pictures up the insides of my thighs. Of what, I can't imagine, but I close my eyes and see them as long, wide streaks of blue paint.

I have shaved for her and for the ocean, short enough that when she runs her tongue along the hairs I know it must prickle her. She uses her tongue on my labia, then parts them, wiggles her way inside, slippery as a fish. Her tongue is a flat brush sweeping the inside of me until she hits my clit. Dot, dot, dabbing me. Her tongue there speaks to me without language. It is a promise of things to come, a press and release that feels as quietly natural as anything that has come before it. There was a time when Helen and I used our tongues like this, on our bodies, instead of against each other....

I brush the thought away. Don't want to think about that right now. Don't want to have to find the words for it.

I fold my body down until I can nestle my own tongue against Margret's bikini bottom. She's still working her tongue against my clit, but I try to focus. I slide her tiny bikini to the side to allow me access. I tuck my finger inside her. She is wet already, smelling of sea salt and musk.

I slide two fingers inside her, loving the wet clutch of her, the way she moans into me. With my thumb rubbing across her clit, I slide a third finger in. I fuck her like that, pushing so hard her tongue slides back and forth across my clit with the movement of her body. Through the wet fabric of her suit, her hard nipples rub my belly with the movement.

Margret arches her back. Her tongue becomes frantic across my clit, and then she gives up and sucks me, hard, into her mouth. We don't come together; she goes first, moaning as I dive into her with my fingers. It is this sound, the meaningless vibrations of her throat as she sucks my clit, that lets me follow her.

The place we bring each other to, there are no words for that.

No words at all.

It is dark when the sound wakes me. Long and loud, like big trucks are driving over the roof of the hut. It takes me a second before I realize what it is. Howler monkeys.

Margret lies awake next to me, her body rigid in my arms.

"Was de hell?" she whispers. At first I think she's speaking English, but then I realize it's just one of those phrases that sound like their English equivalents. It still amazes me sometimes how similar languages are, even after hundreds of years and thousands of miles apart. Languages are a species like any other, I guess, each adapting to its environment, but most still keeping their roots. Some even growing more and more alike over the passing years, despite every hypothesis that says they shouldn't.

I could say, "Howler monkeys," but I know she won't understand, so instead I pull her close to me. I say with my body, "It's safe," and then I kiss her so she'll know for sure.

But her mouth is set flat against mine, and her lips don't open. She is letting me hold her, but she is not relaxed. The moon peeks through the open slats around the top of the hut, and I can see her eyes, big and wide.

The sound comes again, closer this time, a big low howl that fills the hut and echoes all around us. If I didn't know what it was, if I hadn't heard howlers before, I'd be going out of my fucking mind too.

"What the fuck was that?" Margret says again, and this time when I understand her, I think that I have suddenly absorbed a new language, through osmosis, while we slept. And then, in another heartbeat, I realize she is speaking English.

She seems to realize it at the same time, and covers her mouth with her fingertips. I let go of her, sit up on the bed.

"Shit," she says through her fingers. "I am so very sorry, Lilla. It was meant to be a surprise that I learn English. I ruin the…surprise."

Hearing her speak makes me feel like I am farther from home than just in another country. I am on another planet, an alternative universe where everything you thought you understood is reversed, a book that is read from right to left, bottom to top.

For once, I can't say anything. All those languages in my head, and I don't have a word. Not one. She meant to surprise me, I see that now. It is a gift she has tried to give me, learning this language, something to bring us closer.

But all I can see are her lips moving. Her tongue is forming words that I do not want to understand. I turn away. She comes behind me and puts her arms around me, but already her fists are closed tight, filling with words.

MICHAEL HEMMINGSON
THE MOMENTS

EVERYTHING IS RELATIVE in the middle of September—for instance, a hotel room in Sebha at four in the morning, after driving from Tripoli. It was the last time Dominique and I had fucked; or the last time I remembered fucking her. I'm not exactly certain.

I had walked around for two hours waiting for her to wake up after the drive.

It was still summer and an unbearable heat radiated everywhere. I wandered the sparsely populated market area, bought a carton of Camels out of the back of a giant, dilapidated truck with Niger plates—smuggled all the way from the coast, I thought.

This had always been a crossroads for everything illegal: drugs, booze, people.

When I returned to our room, Dominique was coming around; no air-con, sweat all over the bed and clothes sticking to her in the wrong places. She was small and dark, with brown eyes and hair, a big smile with a lot of white teeth. She had been in some real shitholes: smuggling drugs to the Zapatistas; working with some kind of cultural group in Vietnam back in '96; sharing a squat in Istanbul with hashish-smoking human rights investigators. She was wicked smart and had a temper. I'd met her my first year of college and I had no idea what she was doing here, with me, at the emptiest end of the Sahara.

—Where you been?

—Around, I said, there's not a lot to see here; we can rest for a day or two, maybe check out that noise the car's making.

The car, a Range Rover of unknown vintage, was falling apart. I had my doubts it would cough along much longer.

I sat down next to her on the narrow bed. She leaned against me and made a face, and I could feel the heat on her skin. I touched her hair and rubbed her neck. We were quiet, and the world was quiet outside; we touched each other and said nothing. She leaned back and began pulling off her shirt; it came off sticky, with a fight. Her small breasts were bare— no bras here in Africa—dark nipples stiffening in the cool predawn breeze that began blowing through the open window like a childhood memory.

I leaned down and began sucking on her little tits.

She was trying to help me pull off my pants, getting everything more tangled. I stood and slid them off. She was naked and watching me. The bed was covered in deep shadows; I couldn't see her face well and I didn't need to. I didn't want to. I lay down on top of her, my hand down between her legs.

—I don't have a condom, I said.

—I don't care, she said.

She arched her hips, wrapped her legs around my waist. I started to fuck her, and the more we fucked, the more wildcat it got. She started to thrash on the bed and make little crying noises so I had to heavily lie on top of her, press her into the bed, stifle her. Didn't want the sex police kicking in the door. I was starting to see that spinning dizziness that meant I was going to come soon. When I did, I thrust hard, and fell back. She rolled away, back into the sheets.

We stayed in town for two days, enough time to buy groceries, fix the arthritic car and make sure the road ahead was clear of drifting sand, land mines, intermittent fighting, all that fun North African stuff. We set out early in the morning for Ghat, the border crossing with Algeria. I wanted to go further south, cross at Tumu, but Dominique had insisted. Wanted to use her French, I guess. I don't like to have serious talks while driving. Casual conversation, that's okay. But these kind of involved, emotional discussions about relationships and sex, lying and betrayal—I'd rather go to some foul-smelling coffee shop and drink mud. It fucks the road up, you miss the curves, don't get the jumps off the line....

The last year, we were living together and it was either her jumping me after she'd drunk too much, or me paying her. I was jerking off four or five times a day because she hadn't been that interested in sex. She had been living in France for the last few months, doing her junior year abroad. I'd had some encounters, but on our small campus, if I fucked anyone, it would be hard to keep it from the general public.

I did get a blow job from a freshman named Rita: long dreadlocks and big tits. She'd sucked me off in the laundry room of my apartment complex and the noise her mouth made competed with the tumbling dryers. She seemed all right, we went for drinks a few times, but then she ran off with the assistant registrar and I never saw her again.

Like Kurt Vonnegut once wrote generations ago: *So it goes.*

I met up with Dominique in Paris; we rented the car, drove down through Italy, caught the ferry to Malta, spent a week in the mild sun and surf, then took the one ferry to Tripoli. We headed for the Atlantic coast of West Africa, somewhere around Lagos. The heat and emptiness recharged our sex; we'd fucked more in the last twelve days than we had in the last twelve months.

We ran into trouble at the Ghat crossing. The oldest story: our papers weren't in order. While I was trying to straighten it out with my bad Arabic, Dominique was talking to three of the border guards. She was actually flirting with them—touching her hair, laughing and bending forward to show a little tit. They kept pressing in closer and closer to her; I could see their hands patting her shoulder; they were complimenting her hair.

The implied danger aroused me. I tried to keep my mind on dealing with the customs guy, but all I could picture was Dominique getting dragged behind the guard shack by these three and getting royally fucked—one in her mouth and the other taking her from behind on the barren sand while the third jerked off in her hair. I was getting hard thinking about it, my dick throbbing in time with the sound of idling car engines.

We finally got everything settled and we were able to drive on.

A few days later the car died, one hundred miles from the coast. We walked for hours, fighting about whose fault it was. When we reached the next village, we were through. She caught the first bus south, and that was that, I never saw her again...

I think.

I'm not sure.

It's all a blur now, like our entire relationship....

Honestly, I can't remember anymore. Maybe it was some new type of hell that I've decided didn't happen. She still lives over there, in Europe. Hotel Terminus, the Klaus Barbie place. Lyon. A mutual friend told me she was marrying some eighteen-year-old German kid with a nine-inch cock.

The strangest thing about the trip is that I never knew where we were. I fixate on *place*; I must know where I am when traveling, a mental reference, a name to access certain files of gray matter. I cannot locate it on any map. No idea where the house was in Marseilles, back when she was going to school; the chapel along the cliffs where we all almost fell off because of the wind. The bar by the docks in Valletta, a 250-pound dog lying in the narrow entrance, too long to step over. I am cartographically fixated.

What I even remember of that whole blurry period is off. Dominique had been late picking me up at the airport; turns out she had gotten drunk with some Belgians and passed out in a bathtub. She showed up after an hour. I was in the airport bar drinking with someone I think was named Marie. Dominique dragged me off and into the Metro, and took me to a hotel room she'd rented so we could spend a night away from her smelly French roommates.

I hadn't gotten laid in months; I don't know about her.

We checked in, walked up to the room, and attacked each other. Seriously, we ripped each other's clothes off, threw each other around the room like POWs being interrogated. Before I knew it I was coming in her mouth; then we switched and I was going down on her, flicking her clit with my tongue, sucking on it hard; she was screaming, bucking, slapping me on the head and telling me to eat her.

We fucked twice, a few positions, nothing too freaky, we were just getting used to each other's movements again, each other's taste and smell and souls....

Later that night, I was drinking a bottle of Red Label with a stranger who was one of her friends; he was manic and frightened me. He was bi, kept rubbing my thigh. I said I was flattered, but not really into it tonight.

The last day Dominique and I were in France, before we left for Africa, I was out with Monsieur Bisexual—his name was Jean. We were having beers with people in a weird and fucked-up neighborhood on the north side of Paris: lots of crumbly buildings. We'd been at it for a while, really tearing into the liquor, sometimes going into the bathroom and smoking hash; everyone was pretty gone, and after a lot of hours went by, the group decided to go home.

Jean pulled me aside.

—Take a walk with me, he said.

He was huge, six-three easy, maybe 230 pounds. I think he was from the far western part of France, Brittany. Dark all over.

—I don't know, Jean, I told him, we're pretty pixilated; maybe we should go back with everyone else.

—Nothing funny; I want to show you something.

I was feeling displaced. We walked for a while, not saying much. It was late and there weren't a lot of people out.

—Sorry about that first night you were here, all that sloppy shit I laid on you, he said.

—Forget about it.

—Do you want another drink?

—Sure.

We went into a small bar and sat along the back wall, drinking Kronenbourg draft. Jean was telling me about his childhood on the coast, his three years in the army. I noticed a woman looking at us from the bar. She was thin and pale, long blonde hair. I noticed a tattoo of a purple koi peeking out from the small of her back. She was wearing jeans and a white tank top.

She smiled, looked away, looked back.

Jean followed my stare.

—You like her?

—Yeah, I said.

Jean was up and moving. He sat next to her, said something quietly. She leaned back and looked at me again; nodded and said something to Jean.

They got up and left.

—What the fucking fuck, I said to no one in particular.

Jean stuck his head back in through the front door of the bar.

—Are you coming or not?

I tossed a few euros on the bar and walked out. They were about ten feet ahead of me, walking side by side down the street. Their hands were resting on each other's asses. I could see Jean's hand squeeze her, pinch her flesh. She jumped, laughed, hit his arm. They sidelined into an alley that ran along a huge building that looked like a hospital.

The woman led Jean down a staircase and onto a small landing. She quickly stripped out of her jeans and tank top. Jean pulled his pants off. She was on her knees, working his balls with her right hand while licking up and down the length of his dick. I have to admit: he had a beautiful cock, long and curved, pretty fat, nice color. I was impressed, not jealous.

I wasn't sure what I was supposed to be doing. My hand went down into my own pants. She was working her left hand around to Jean's asshole; I could see the fingers slide into his crack, and when I saw his body stiffen I knew she was probing that pucker. Jean looked over at me, glassy-eyed.

—Take them off, he said.

I unbuckled, slid my pants down around my boots and kind of walk-shuffled over to them. The woman let go of Jean's balls and grabbed mine. She popped his cock all the way into her mouth and really jammed two of her fingers into his ass. Jean was pumping, fucking this woman's mouth, moving between her fingers and mouth like he was an engine. When he came, I thought I could hear it splash against her throat. She pulled back and started in on my cock without a word. I really wanted to fuck her; she was too quick for me. I came almost immediately; Jean watched closely and rubbed my neck as this anonymous girl drank everything I gave her, slurping noisily while her fingers started playing with my asshole.

I sat down on a garbage can and tried to recover my wits as she wiped her lips and face with a handkerchief. Jean pulled out a wad of bills from his pocket, counted off a few, gave them to her. She kissed us both on the cheek, and then walked away.

Jean and I sat there.

—I won't say anything to Dominique, he said.

—There's really no reason not to.

—I think she would be more upset by my being here than by you getting sucked off by a common *sale putain*, he said.

—Yeah? I said.

—She is tired of me seeing her friends' cocks, he said with a shrug.

—I'm sure, I said.

He laughed and then I laughed, too.

—That's her, I said.

—That *is* our Dominique, he said.

We had a moment, laughing and patting each other on the back, and then we stood up and left the alley.

RAKELLE VALENCIA

LINE SHACK

VERY FALL THEY HAD MET for an overnight at the line shack to put in supplies and ready the small place for a cowboy to lay up while tending fence over the harsh winter. She would arrive from town, driving the old ranch pickup as far as it would go into the mountainous terrain, while he took the route along the fence, leading her mare and a pack mule with flopping panniers, only stopping to make repairs to the barbed wire as needed.

The early morning sun glinted off of the dew that dangled precariously from the wire, letting Flint know that the lines were up and taut for as far as he could see. The colt under him set a quick pace in the chill with the mare only too happy to trot up, but the mule pulled back now and again in protest.

Flint squirmed and adjusted his seat on the hard, worn buckaroo saddle, uncomfortable with his growing need and the anticipation. He pulled at his collar as if that would help, then checked his hold on the dallying mule. He had set out before the sun had even blazed its red streaks through the mountain crags, anxious to meet up with the battered truck that would stop in Vaca Rojo Pass.

The rope across his right thigh tightened, indenting into his chaps. Flint prepared a second ahead of the mule's antics as it let out a series of unbroken brays and crow-hopped its protest to the lengthy jaunt. It would become more cantankerous when loaded down with supplies, but even the thought of an unruly mule didn't relieve the pressure in the crotch of his Wranglers.

Flint's physical discomfort tugged his mind from the mule's all-too-normal behavior and made him ponder ways of relief. He squirmed within the saddle again, the friction causing an even worse problem. If he stopped to dismount and take the matter into his own hands, he would be late. Not to mention that he might lose the mule with his momentary lack of attention and no place to tie off the strong animal. No, he would keep riding. But something would have to be done before the few hours' ride to the line shack.

The cotton briefs and his jeans chafed his trapped cock. He swore to himself, feeling like sandpaper was rasping at his dick with every forward movement of the jog. He asked his colt to lengthen its stride as he began to post the gait, affording a small comfort.

Vaca Rojo Pass would come within his sight over the next ridge, which would, Flint knew, increase his engorging problem tenfold. Just the vision of her... Just the knowing that she waited in the rusted old truck for him...

The sun didn't bother to gleam off of the pitted chrome, but the truck sat with its engine running, waiting nonetheless. Flint cantered the last half mile then let the horses walk the last forty feet. They weren't blowing or sweating, so he took no mind to walking them out longer.

He gingerly stepped down from his colt like a bowlegged old man stiff with the cold. She killed the engine, then got out of the truck, slammed the door and leaned against it with a grin that told him she knew.

Bending down, he hobbled both horses and removed their bridles in turn. The mule was dragged to the hitch at the back of the truck and tied off tight using a quick-release knot in case the beast decided to somehow rampage the dented vehicle. He turned toward her then. "Is that all you can do is grin?"

She eyed him up and down, then stared at the bulge pressing outward beneath worn jeans from the front gap in his chaps.

"Lady," he continued, "you did this to me."

She laughed. "Can't you wait?"

"I've been waitin'. And it has been miserable."

She gave him a look, then hopped onto the hood of the truck that had been warmed by the engine, sitting on exposed hands. Flint tossed the bridles onto the seat of the cab before walking to the front of the vehicle and wrapping his arms around her waist, sliding her into him where her legs had to part and her pussy rested against his flat belly.

She bent to kiss him. What was supposed to be a quick hello turned into ravenous sucking and tongue twisting. Her hands found his neck, and she entwined fingers in his unruly brown hair shot with the beginnings of silver, knocking the wool-felted Stetson forward.

Flint removed his hat, then began working at pulling off her boots as they continued to kiss.

"Hey," she said, "you really can't wait."

He growled in answer, recapturing her lips with his own to nibble and suck. The second boot was shucked easily and left to drop to the hardening ground with a thud. Reaching for her jeans, she helped him pluck the button and drag the zipper down. Then she wiggled as he tugged at her pants to get them out of his way, panties tangled within.

His own gritty zipper complained, but he managed to fight it open. With relief, his hard-on sprang out, liberated from several layers of cotton confinement.

She reached for him. Flint evaded her touch, fisting his prick in his own familiar hand while pushing her backward to lie on the hood with his other. His rod twitched as his nostrils caught the musky scent that told of her own excitement. He placed his full palm over her entire pussy, pressuring with the heel of his hand in tiny circles over the mons.

He felt her wetness and replaced his hand with his mouth. The tip of his tongue touched within her slit to trace her clit shaft before he spread her nether lips with his fingers and lapped the length of her in rhythm.

Her pelvis rose to meet him as he switched to perform circles around her clit. He yanked his head from her clenching fingers and said, "Darling, I need this now." With both hands, he slid her body to meet the tip of his steely hard-on. She gasped while her short nails squealed along the red paint searching for purchase in the smooth metal. Flint fisted his dick again and thrust upward at that moment.

He pushed his rod in to the hilt only to drag himself halfway out and slam back in fast.

He needed this.

He needed to get off.

He needed the relief she could give him.

His calloused thumb pad now circled her clit while he rammed into her repeatedly. She moaned and gasped, crying out incoherently. Her eyes squeezed shut as her mouth contorted and her facial expressions became surreal, as if some alien beast inhabited her.

Flint knocked into her faster and faster, unwilling to slow his pounding, losing himself in the feel of her. But she was the first to cry out, surprising him. Flint had felt his need was greater than her own when he arrived. His could be seen so clearly. He hadn't stopped to think that she had also waited too long and might have driven the rocky pathway in discomfort, too.

Wave after wave of her orgasm gripped and sucked at him. Her legs wrapped around him to hold him more tightly into her. That was his undoing. That last slam, powered by the force of muscular, feminine thighs brought him to his limits. His upper body crumpled onto her, neither one moving while the aftershocks of their fucking continued to rumble through them.

It felt like a glorious eternity, but it had only been mere minutes that they stayed locked with each other. Flint adjusted himself, then zipped up, reaching next to help his wife with her clothes and boots.

"Best get the mule loaded if we're to make the line shack before nightfall."

"Mmm," she hummed, still basking in that freshly fucked glow.

Flint busied himself unloading the truck and arranging the cans, boxes and bags into the panniers hanging from either side of the mule's sawbuck. When she could, his wife bridled then released the hobbles from the horses for the next leg of their journey. Then she mounted her mare and held the colt steady while Flint dragged the mule over and stepped up.

The mountainous terrain grew precarious but the wire fence was unbothered, needing no repairs, probably because this pasture was only used during the cold season where the mountains would block the harshest bite of winter. And where cattle could still scrub the dead forage.

Several hours later, they both arrived at the line shack weary yet excited. Putting in supplies each year was like playing at house in the heyday of the cowboys and cattle drives. This one night was their vacation for the year, before the cowboy who wrangled fence all winter would move in and set the place his own way.

It took both of them to haul the full panniers into the one-room shack. Then she shoved wood into the potbellied stove while he untacked the horses and mule and put them in the corral, rubbing them with a curry. He fed them grain from the supplies and threw them a bale from the small barn that had been stocked during haying season last summer.

Carrying the saddle blankets, bridles, hobbles, halter and lead rope to the house, Flint almost jolted the door into his wife as she hung the rifle above the frame. She backed away and finished her unpacking by stowing the boxes of cartridges on a nearby shelf, then hanging the bag of hardtack from one of the old rod-iron hooks bolted to a ceiling beam.

Hardtack used to be a staple but was now only carried in saddlebags in case of an emergency. Today there were canned foods and ground coffee, boxes of pasta and other dry goods, and jars of sauces, almost everything a regular house pantry would hold. Refrigeration was remiss but there was plenty of heat for cooking on the woodstove, and there would be water in snowfall after the initial bottled gallons ran out.

Finished, she wiped her hands down the sides of her jeans. Flint wrapped his arms around her from behind in a bear hug as he tried to pull her to the bed. She broke loose and stooped to pick up both sets of figure-eight hobbles.

She reached for Flint's wrists in turn, securing each in a hobble, then easily led him to where she hung the hobbles on the old, empty hardtack hooks. His arms were spread sufficiently. He had to rock to the balls of his feet to keep the leather hobbles from digging in.

His wife walked around him, surveying his bondage and helplessness. When she returned to the front of him, she ripped open his yoked cowboy shirt, thrilling in the tinny sound of those pearly snaps cutting loose. She ran a cool hand across his bare chest, following the ridges of his hard pectorals and resting in the nest of light brown curls at the center as she tongued first one flattened nipple, then the other.

Flint moaned with the warm ministrations until he felt her teeth clamp to the risen right nipple. Shock shot through him, mentally and physically. Shifting around in erotic exquisiteness, he inadvertently dropped to his heels. Immediately, he felt the leather tighten around his wrists to bite in, and noticed a burning stretching down his arms. He popped back to the balls of his feet, almost to his toes for relief, thrusting his pelvis forward in the motion.

His wife tore open his jeans and yanked them to his thighs, capturing and controlling his legs. From her back pocket, she fetched her lock-back blade and knifed through his sensible, white cotton briefs from the front of each upper thigh to his waistband. Flint dipped his head to watch in tension as the sharp blade drove past his tenting prick on either side, all too close for his taste.

The briefs fell apart with the spring of his loosed hard-on. She rubbed the cold steel along the bottom of its length then palmed his dick to his belly as she shaved the knife over his balls, curls falling to the floor. "Babe," he said. "Hon?"

She wasn't listening. Flint sought to unhook his wrists, but he had already done himself in when he had dropped to his heels and allowed the bindings to grow taut. She would have to release him. But she hadn't listened to his plea.

Her hand around his cock began jerking him slowly as she closed her knife and shoved it into her back pocket once again. Her other hand now clasped his balls, sending Flint sensations he had never previously felt. The newly exposed skin quivered with her touch. And he jumped when her hot tongue bathed the shorn area. He was close now. So close. Flint clenched his jaw and bucked forward as far as his restraints would allow.

He shoved himself to his toes to thrust his prick into her mouth, emitting a low, guttural, savage growl as he came. Slouching limply on his bonds, he felt her sting his ass with a slap so that he would rise to his toes while she freed the hobbles from the hooks.

Flint hugged his wife close, their mouths leisurely kissing.

He was free now, but the memories of the bondage remained.

KIS Lee

BUS RIDE

VEN THOUGH I COULD HAVE DRIVEN to Vegas, I was going to take the bus this year. Downtown Los Angeles to Las Vegas—forty dollars for a round-trip from a tour company in Chinatown. With the recent hike in gas prices, I couldn't find a better deal.

It was a last-minute trip. An old college friend was going to elope to the original Elvis wedding chapel, and she needed an extra bridesmaid. As long as I didn't need a taffeta dress, I couldn't say no to Vegas. I packed my party clothes and headed out to Chinatown around seven thirty a.m.

Since it was a midweek trip, I didn't expect a big crowd. When I arrived I saw about twenty or so elderly Asians waiting for the bus. After buying my ticket, I stood in line with the rest of the crowd. A few older women acknowledged me, but mostly they kept to themselves. They probably thought I was a college student on vacation.

I chose a seat toward the back of the bus, close to the only bathroom. With stops, the trip to Vegas would take about five hours. By car, I could do the trip in about four, but this way I could relax during the ride and catch up on work.

I looked up when I saw a pair of legs in my peripheral vision. A tall Asian man looked down at me and grinned. "Is this seat taken?"

I noticed that the bus wasn't even half full yet. Most of the passengers had accumulated in the middle, with only a few middle-aged couples toward the back. I thought the young man could take another seat, but I wasn't in the mood to argue. I grunted a response and removed my backpack.

"Thanks," he said. He sat down and stretched his long legs in front of him. He was close to six feet, with a lean build. He wore his hair short, and I wondered vaguely if he'd spent time in the military. I waited to see if he put his bag under his seat, but he only carried a leather jacket folded in his lap.

He looked at me and smiled again. His dark lashes framed his deep brown eyes. "I'm sorry to intrude," he said. "I'm tired, and I don't want to be sitting next to a nosy Chinese grandmother."

I had to smile back. "I know what you mean. Do you speak Chinese?"

"Yes and no. Enough to get by, but I'm not fluent." He cocked his head while looking at me. "Are you Chinese?"

"I'm a Korean-Chinese mutt," I said. "I'm Amanda, by the way."

His warm hand completely covered mine. "Dave."

After a bit of introductory chitchat, we settled in our seats. He leaned his seat back and closed his eyes. As the bus rolled away from the station, I reached down for my backpack. I grazed his leg and mumbled, "Excuse me." He didn't respond, so I assumed he was out.

I graded papers for about forty minutes until the motion of the bus made me queasy. Then I stared outside the window and watched the cars below us. I heard my seatmate shift his legs.

"Are you a teacher?" he asked.

I smiled. "I thought you were sleeping."

"I was just resting my eyes," he said. "Do you teach high school?"

"I teach sixth grade for now. It's a temporary gig while I work on my book."

He studied me with half-closed eyes. "A writer. I think I can see that. With those Lisa Loeb glasses, you have that artsy vibe coming from you."

I shrugged. Most people usually assumed I was a student. Probably because of my glasses and the fact that I hardly ever wore makeup. I kept my straight hair in a simple ponytail. Except for special occasions, I almost always wore a T-shirt and jeans. To be comfortable for the ride, I had worn my black sweatpants that day.

"So what are you writing about?"

I had expected that question. Usually, I give a generic answer. This time, I looked him right in the eyes and said, "I write smut."

He raised his eyebrows. "Do you really?"

I nodded, waiting for his reaction. He studied my face, his eyes wandering to my collarbone. His attention went back to my eyes as if he thought he could see something in them. Even though he showed a small smile, his eyes remained neutral.

"Are there any Asian-American writers in the smut business?" he asked. "You could be the Amy Tan of the porn world."

I laughed. That was the same thing my roommate had told me. I looked up when the bus slowed down for the first stop. I waited for Dave to leave his seat and followed him off the bus.

After using the restroom, I wandered to the other side of the bus. I wanted to smoke but not in front of the Asian grandmothers. As I lit up, I watched Dave leave the restroom. He stretched his arms over his head and looked up toward the sky. I don't usually go for clean-cut men, but I decided to make an exception. There was something about his eyes that made me want to know him better.

I returned to my seat while the others chatted outside. I opened my backpack to make sure my dress wasn't too wrinkled. Velvet usually travels well, but I didn't want to take my chances. I should have brought a suitcase, but I was averse to carrying around any bulky luggage. Moving the dress out of the way, I searched for my accessory case.

"Are you looking for this?"

Dave tossed my velvet choker on my lap. "You dropped this on your way out."

My face burned as I shoved it back into my bag. It was a simple black choker with a silver hook in front.

He sat next to me again. His forearm barely brushed mine as he leaned toward me. "So what's the collar for? Your lover?"

I didn't look away from his probing eyes. "I don't know what you mean. It's just a necklace," I lied.

His dark eyes twinkled as he put a finger to his lips. He winked and leaned back in his seat.

I sat still and stared at the window. We were back on the highway, and neither of us said a word. I listened to snippets of conversations.

— 46 —

Some passengers were going to visit family members. Others were eager to try their chances at the slot machines. The gentle rocking made my head throb, and I closed my eyes.

I woke up to a hand tapping my shoulder. Disoriented, I jumped away from the touch. I looked over and saw Dave's smiling face. He held his hands up, showing me his palms.

"We're in Barstow," he said. "It's probably the last rest stop before we hit Vegas. I didn't think you'd want to miss that."

I rubbed sleep out of my eyes. "Thanks." I went to the restroom to splash some cold water on my face. The nap had gotten rid of the motion sickness, and I felt refreshed and ready for Vegas.

Dave was waiting for me when I got back. He shifted his legs to the side, and I climbed over them. I noticed how nice his long legs looked in denim. I've always loved a man who looks good in jeans.

"You never told me what the collar is for," he said. He blocked my exit with his legs.

I hesitated. I could have told him to fuck off and mind his own business. But something let me know that his question was more than mere curiosity. I stood up to see how many others were on the bus. It wasn't too late to find another seat.

"Sit down," he said. He never raised his voice, but I complied. He smiled when I sat down. His dark eyes locked on to mine.

"Don't be shy, love. Tell me why you need a collar."

"It's for a party," I said. "My friend is getting married, and we're going out clubbing afterward."

"I see." He ran his hand over my thigh, his fingertips hovering in the air, never touching the soft fabric. He had large hands with long fingers. Whenever I saw a man with long fingers, I wondered if he knew how to play the piano.

He moved his hand from my thigh to my forearm, lightly brushing my bare skin with his fingertips. His touch went from the inside of my wrist to my elbow and up toward my bicep, stroking my skin slowly like he was memorizing my texture. I watched his gaze slide over my breasts, my stomach, and lower.

When the bus rolled into motion, I jumped. I hadn't even heard the driver announce our departure. Shifting in my seat, I noticed that all the passengers had congregated around the front and middle. A few middle-aged ladies were discussing which casino had the best buffet.

"No one can see us," Dave whispered.

I stared into his eyes. I thought about how he kept using the word *collar*. Was he interested in the scene? He seemed so clean-cut and vanilla. Then again, so did I. He removed his hand from my arm.

"Do you want me to stop?"

I shook my head.

"I'm not going to hurt you," he said. "Are you willing to trust me?"

He looked so solemn. My curiosity won, and I nodded.

"Good." He leaned over me and pressed the button on my arm rest. I breathed in his scent of soap and tobacco as he pressed my seat back to match the angle of his own.

His face was so close to mine that I expected him to kiss me. I held my breath and turned my face toward him. He smiled and cupped my right breast. When I gasped, he squeezed me tightly, making my nipple hard. Watching my face, he moved his hand to my other breast. He played with my nipple, pinching it between his thumb and forefinger. I saw his lips twist into a smile.

I looked around to see if anyone was near. He grabbed my chin with one hand and said, "Don't worry about anything else." Then he turned his body toward me and moved his hand under my shirt. His hand felt warm beneath my bra. With his other hand, he undid the snap. "Take that off and give it to me."

I slipped the straps out of my sleeves and removed my bra. I was embarrassed that I wasn't wearing something sexier. Instead of something lacy, I wore one made of plain cotton.

He smiled when he saw it. "Plain and no-nonsense. I like that about you. Turn and face the window."

I did what he said. When he placed my hands behind my back, my mouth went dry, and I licked my lips. He used my bra to tie my wrists together, taking his time, making a tight knot. I knew I wouldn't be able to wear that bra again.

"Face forward."

I sat with my hands behind my back. He draped his jacket over my shoulders.

"We have a while until we reach Vegas," he said. "Let's see if we can make the time go faster."

His right hand slipped into the waistband of my pants. I was glad that I had worn pants with a drawstring waist. He smiled when he touched my panties.

"White cotton?"

"Yes," I said.

His finger touched my clit. I spread my thighs wider to give him better access. His middle finger slid past my clit and played with my opening. I sighed as he massaged my pussy lips. He hooked his finger and entered me in one slow movement. A second finger followed, and I squirmed on the seat.

He fucked me slowly with two fingers while his palm pressed against my clit. I arched my back to take his fingers deeper. He remained impassive with his eyes closed—his reflection flickered in the window before me—and his fingers buried inside me while I ground myself against his hand.

His fingers slid out of me, and he concentrated on my clit. He rubbed me with his fingertips, faster, until I was breathing hard. Shifting his position, he slid his other hand into my pants. While he rubbed my clit with one hand, he finger-fucked me with the other. Right before I came, he turned my head back and kissed me hard, slipping his tongue into my mouth just as he entered me with a third finger. My muscles clenched around his hand, and I moaned into his mouth, shaking.

He licked my bottom lip and smiled. "We're here."

"Already?" I thought only fifteen minutes had passed, but we'd been playing for over an hour. My hands felt numb behind my back. "Are you going to untie me now?"

"Not yet." His grin sent a shiver through me.

The bus rolled to a stop, and he grabbed my backpack. With his jacket still around my shoulder, I walked off the bus. He led us to the back of the bus station, away from the waiting area. Then he took off the jacket and released my arms.

Without a word, he turned me around and placed my palms against the wall. The Vegas heat made the brick burning hot, but I didn't complain. With one smooth movement, he slid my pants down to my ankles. I listened to the sounds of his zipper coming down and then the condom wrapper being tossed aside.

He raised my hips until he found the angle he liked, then eased his cock forward. Even though I was still wet, he took his time. He was thick, and it was a tight fit. We both sighed when he was completely inside me.

His first few strokes were soft, but then his thrusts became faster. His fingers dug into my hips as he fucked me hard. When I looked over my shoulder to see if anyone was coming, he grabbed my pony-tail and forced me to stare at the wall. When he was close, he pulled my hair all the way back until I was looking toward the desert sun. He groaned and shuddered against me. My legs trembled as I held on to the wall for support. He pulled my pants back up and smoothed the fabric over my legs. He grinned as he picked up my torn bra. Shoving it in his back pocket, he said, "A souvenir."

We didn't exchange numbers. We kissed good-bye and went our separate ways. I arrived at my friend's hotel with an obvious smile on my face. She wanted details, but we had a bachelorette party to attend.

The wedding was beautiful. The bride looked fabulous in her red dress, and the groom went all out in a white tuxedo. We partied afterward until five in the morning. After a two-hour nap, I went to call a cab.

The bride gave me a hug outside the hotel. "Are you sure you don't want to ride back with us? We're leaving for L.A. the day after tomorrow."

"I have to teach in the morning. Plus my ticket was round-trip—and forty bucks."

She laughed. "Forty bucks for a round-trip. Who would've thought? That's a sweet deal."

"Indeed."

I arrived at the station early. When I boarded the bus, I walked toward the back. Dave looked up from his newspaper and smiled. "How was the wedding?"

"Perfect," I said. I climbed over his lap and settled in my seat. I tossed a black velvet bag onto his lap. "From the bachelorette party."

He peered inside and touched the soft hemp rope. Dug deeper and found the blindfold and the other items. He laughed when he saw the stubby miniature flogger. "Cute. It's travel sized. So you never told me about the subject of your book."

"I'm writing about bondage. I'm currently in the research stage." I wondered what he would think about my new bra: pink with lace around the cups.

I had five hours to find out.

MATHILDE MADDEN

WET

EARLY EVENING. Getting dark.

Michael's hands are at a perfect ten to two on the steering wheel. The car whips along the M40, taking us nearer to home every moment. The kids have both been asleep in the back for over an hour, and I'm fading in and out myself, listening to the low murmur of Radio Four, watching the kaleidoscope patterns of the orange streetlights. Drifting.

Michael doesn't know I'm still awake. I haven't said anything for a while and he isn't looking at me, just straight out at the darkening motorway. Steely eyed and rigid jawed. He might like to be a bit of a boy racer when he's on his own, but he doesn't mess about when he's driving his family. Protecting his family is who he is.

It's not raining right now. Typical. Because it rained for the entire week we were in the Lakes. Every type of rain from drenching sheets to the lightest, featherlike drizzle. Michael and I had to spent our days hunting for indoor child-friendly activities, our evenings fighting over who had to crouch under a waterproof cape and cook sausages and our nights listening to rain on canvas and trying not to make too much noise as we pressed close and warm in the dark. Michael was the one who said camping in autumn half term was too chancy, weather-wise. Especially in the Lakes. But to his credit, he bore the worst the holiday threw at him with typical stalwart grace.

Before we had kids we never used to go camping. But then having kids is a brave new world. In truth, a change of holiday destinations barely blips the radar when you're faced with all the upheaval of starting a family. But once upon a time we went to Ibiza and danced the night away—back when that was a fashionable thing to do. We went to Barbados on honeymoon, even though we couldn't really afford it. We had one of those all-inclusive deals with meals and drinks and Jet Skis thrown in. And we wasted most of it, because we never left our room for the entire fortnight.

Except for the room service. We got our money's worth there. For the first three days we lived on champagne, strawberries and chocolate. Oh, and love.

It's about eight o'clock when we break the journey at my parents' place near Banbury. Keswick to Brighton is too much to do in one go. Even after dark with the kids fast asleep. We crunch up the gravel drive of the house I grew up in. Even after all these years, it still feels like coming home.

Later, when the kids have been deposited—still sleeping—into the beds in my parents' spare room, my mum says, "Why don't you two go down to the pub in the village for a quick drink? I bet you didn't get any time to yourselves all holiday."

It's only nine o'clock, but we're both tired. Even so, a bit of adult time is very appealing. Michael looks at me and I look at him. The children are so sound asleep they didn't even stir when we lifted them out of their car seats.

"Thanks, Mum," I say, pulling a couple of notes out of my handbag and stuffing them into the back pocket of Michael's jeans.

By the time we're at the end of the drive, we're practically running toward the prospect of adult conversation and draft lager.

The pub in the village is tiny. More someone's front room than a real pub. Quaint is the word, I guess. But, to me, it's just the local pub I grew up with, so I have to see it through a stranger's eyes to really notice how chocolate-box cozy it is, with its armchairs and its roaring fire and its red-nosed patrons.

Michael grins at the sight of this parochial place. He always finds my Oxfordshire country-bumpkin origins funny—being such a city boy himself. Fields and mud and cow dung, so not his thing. Another reason why he's such a hero for going camping in October.

He takes off his glasses—it's cold enough outside that they've steamed up in the pub—and pulls the edge of his T-shirt out and polishes the lenses. I catch a tiny glimpse of his hard stomach as he does so. And moments later, as he leans over the bar, I watch the way his jeans hug his arse. I want to run over and grab hold of it. Bite it. Ten years on, he still has the body I married.

I can't help it then. I keep thinking about his body. By the time he sets the two pints of lager down on the table, I'm imagining him naked. Thinking about his cock in my mouth or in my pussy. I swallow, look up at him, smile, wonder if he can read my mind. But he doesn't say anything.

It's midweek, but the pub has a pretty healthy smattering of people. It's a friendly place, but no one pays us any attention. It's as if they know how little time we get alone together. Somehow, it's as intimate as it would be if it were just the two of us alone somewhere.

Over the top of his glass, Michael smiles warmly at me and my heart leaps. Somehow this cozy pub, this little oasis from our day-to-day lives of family and work and muddy camping in the rain, feels more romantic than an all-inclusive Barbados resort or dancing 'til dawn in an aircraft-hangar-sized nightclub.

Michael takes a long pull of his pint. I bite my lip. His mouth is so pretty. I reach out and wipe a little foam off his top lip. He smiles again.

"Michael," I say, "are you thinking what I'm thinking?"

"Possibly," says Michael. "If what you're thinking is how gorgeous my wife is."

We finally roll out of the pub at one a.m. Licensing laws don't seem to be too strictly applied out here in the middle of nowhere.

We're dizzy and laughing after a few hours of drinking and teasing and playing footsie under the table. For a few moments we don't even notice that it's raining again. Heavily. Big fat drops are splattering the pavement. Splattering us, too. We're not dressed for it. We've just spent a week swathed in waterproofs, but tonight we walked out of my mum and dad's house in jeans and sweats. We could go back into the pub, but it's so late and we've still got a fair bit of driving to do in the morning. Michael's sandy hair is already starting to stick to his face as he stands there. I take his hand. "Come on," I say, "I know a shortcut."

The path over the fields and through the woods is unlit, but there's a big bright harvest moon in the sky. Locally this path is known as Muddy Lane. Never more aptly named than now. Two weeks of rain and now this downpour has created a swamp. We slip and slide in the dark, laughing and cursing equally, struggling not to lose our balance or our shoes as we cling to each other and squelch through the mire.

We're about halfway home when Michael stops. "Hang on a minute," he says, panting. "I can't see a thing." He ducks under a soggy tree and pulls off his glasses. He uses a T-shirt corner again to wipe away the raindrops. I gaze at him, lit perfectly by the big fat moon hanging in the sky. Raindrops are dripping from his hair onto his face as he concentrates on the job in hand. They glitter like sequins, caught in his grazing of stubble. Who knows what possesses me to do what I do next? Maybe it's disco fever. I lean over and lick a little drop of water that is squiggling its way down his jawline.

In less than a heartbeat, Michael turns his head and catches my mouth with his. His arms are round me. His glasses are gone. Where? In his pocket? Actually, I don't care. I open my mouth underneath his and my whole body turns as soft and pliable as cookie dough as he pushes me up against the tree trunk.

Michael kisses me over and over. It feels like everything happens at once. Time and motion stop making sense. His tongue is in my mouth, his teeth are worrying my ear, his lips are caressing my neck.

I work my hands up inside his shirt and tweak and pinch his nipples, making him gasp. His body feels so beautiful beneath my hands. Hard and smooth and hot. I slide my hands lower down to find he's hard and smooth and hot in other places, too. His lips and teeth are still tracing knee-weakening patterns on the angles between my neck and my shoulder. I can feel his light stubble there, too, prickling me like hundreds of tiny kisses.

I slide my hands around and down the back of his jeans, grabbing his arse like I wanted to do in the pub. It's even better than I imagined. High and firm and...oh God, I want to see him naked. I want to taste him. Press my mouth on him. Feel his skin, his heat, his delicious need.

Twisting the two of us around, so he's the one with his back pressed against the tree trunk, I bring my hands round to the front of his jeans and start to undo them. It takes forever. What he's still doing to my neck makes it hard to concentrate. But I manage. I get his jeans off. And his underwear. His cock springs into my hands. Hard and unnaturally warm in the damp night air. I press close to him so he can rub against my leg. He moans deep in his throat and I gasp.

I untangle myself from him and slide to my knees in the mud. The ground is cold, but my desire and the heat pulsing from his body keep me warm. His cock is damp with pre-come. There's a little droplet on the tip, sparkling in the moonlight, just like the glittering raindrops earlier.

Beyond the canopy of the tree's branches the rain slows and starts to stop. I can hear owls hooting and distant traffic noise. I lick the little drop of moisture from the tip of Michael's cock. It tastes like a drop of water from a distant ocean. I remember standing on the balcony of our hotel room in Barbados —looking out over the glassy sea—a million years ago. Michael was the one on his knees that time. Hidden by the balcony. Pressing his tongue against my pussy as I looked out to sea. Out at the sea we never so much as dipped a toe into, because we were too busy diving into each other.

Michael groans again. One of his big, elegant hands tangles in my damp hair. I sigh and let him push me close to his straining cock, opening my mouth. I suck hard, taking him down my throat as far as I can. It's difficult to imagine now, but before I met Michael, I never really liked sucking cock all that much. It was always just a duty— something I did purely for the payback. But with him it's so different. With him, even when we first met, it was almost like giving him pleasure was as much for me as it was for him. The way he moans. The way he thrusts. The way he wants. He gives so much back. It's like feedback then—his arousal flowing into mine taking me higher and higher. As I listen to the noises he makes, I work harder: touching his more sensitive spots with my tongue; using my throat, the sides of my cheeks, and getting rewarded as he gets more and more desperate.

Before he comes, Michael pushes me away, pulls me to my feet and takes his turn taking off *my* trousers. I'm wearing sweatpants, so it's a quick enough job to get them down my legs. They're caked with mud at the bottoms though, so there's no way they're coming right off without a fight. I manage to get one foot free, losing a shoe somewhere in the tangle of mud and combed jersey. That's enough.

With my back pressed up against the trunk of the tree, he lifts me, holding me up long enough to get his cock in position, and then he lets me slide down on to it. I've never done it like this before. Standing up. Never ever. I freeze for a moment. Unsure. A little scared of the way that gravity is driving the penetration so deep. But then as I relax into it and the sensations wash over me, I squirm. It's delicious. I find a slightly better angle and cry out. Michael's mouth finds that sweet spot on my neck again and he nips me hard. I buck and we both nearly topple over. Then his mouth finds mine and we hit a rhythm.

It's hard to balance, though. It's even more difficult for Michael, who is having to support some of my weight as only my toes graze the ground. But the way I sucked his cock, until he was teetering on the edge of orgasm, means he's already close to coming now. He only has to thrust inside me once, twice, before I feel him start to come as his knees buckle and we tumble to the ground….

The tree branches are still dripping, even though the rain has stopped. Water splashes down on my face. It's probably wetter here, under the tree, than outside in the lane now. Wetter still now Michael is on top of me, kissing his way down my muddy half-dressed body. I look at him. He's filthy, too. Muddier than he ever got on our wet weekend of camping. He looks like he'll never be clean again. I kind of like that.

His kiss-kiss trail reaches my stomach and travels over it to my hips. It reaches the place where my inner thighs, my lower abdomen and my pussy all become one. The very center of me. His tongue works lower, deeper, getting closer and closer to the wettest place of all.

I gasp and tighten. Buck and roll. He puts both hands on my hips to still me and presses further on. His tongue finds my clit. Flick-flick. I reach down and push my fingers into his damp hair, tracing patterns on his skull that seem to find their way straight through him to the patterns he traces on my pussy. While his tongue is on my clit, I can feel his sharply stubbled chin against my vagina, prickling that sensitive place just over the edge of pain. It's sparky sharp. Points of light, of heat, of pleasure. I twist against it.

More.

Did I say that out loud? I'm not even sure, but somehow Michael responds. The lazy circles his tongue was drawing around my clit get faster, harder. He presses closer to me. I let go of his hair and my hands scrabble in the cold muddy earth. When I come, I open my eyes and, through the tree canopy, I really do see stars….

We're giggling like teenagers as I put my key in the lock of my mum and dad's house. I don't know what I'll say if they're not in bed. We both look like refugees from Glastonbury—head to toe mud. I never did find that shoe again.

Luckily, the house is silent. We creep up into the bathroom. In steamy warmth, we shower away the debris of our alfresco fun, kissing and caressing as we do. Michael grabs the soap and rubs suds over my body, tweaking my nipples and massaging my arse. I have to press close against him and draw him into a long kiss to keep quiet. His body is so firm and smooth, lubricated by the warm soapy water. Pressed together we slide around, luxuriating in each other. I end up coming again, pressed up against the slickly tiled wall as Michael works his fingers between my legs. We're soaking wet again, but this time it's warm and clean and we're breathless with our need to keep quiet.

I drift downstairs the next morning, still daydreaming about last night's adventure. I glance into the living room and see that the kids are breakfasted and watching cartoons. My mum is in the kitchen washing up cereal bowls. I grab some tea from the pot to wake myself up.

"Thanks for sorting the kids out," I say. "You didn't have to. You could have woken me up."

Mum turns and smiles, wiping her hands on a tea towel. "I thought I'd let you two sleep in after getting caught in that rainstorm. You had quite a night of it, I understand. You two dirty devils."

I nearly spit out my tea. "What?"

Mum smiles. She nods over at the hallway. I must have come downstairs half-asleep because I never even noticed the trail of mud and dirty water that leads from the front door all the way upstairs to the bathroom.

"Oh right. Dirty devils. Yeah, sorry about that, Mum."

T. C. CaLLIGaRI

HeaT

VERYTHING WAS TOO HOT. Erica had been in Mexico City for six months working as an English language teacher and she had had no time to cool down. The sweltering heat, the oppressive smog and the overall grayness of one of the biggest cities on earth weighed upon her. But she had been too busy to unwind. Between the divorce, the new job, and trying to implement a change in the immersion class at the college, Erica hadn't even explored the museum or the zócalo.

And it was so hot.

It was as if a great slab weighed her down, partially melting her, partially keeping her below the boiling point, without any sign of release. Every night, she would finally get home after the interminably long day and subway ride with only enough energy to eat and crawl into bed. Several times, Erica had tried to release the burgeoning need within her, to alleviate the stress with a bit of solo sexual pleasure (the sex was the only part of her marriage that she missed). But the few times she'd tried, she had fallen asleep with her hands between her legs, unsated, with the greater need for sleep winning.

Need and heat built in her every day, making her agitated and short tempered, and she could little afford that with a new job in a foreign city. But there was no time for her gratification—not until the course was in place, and that would be another six months of ironing out the kinks.

Erica sighed, pulling back her blonde hair as she waited for the subway train to arrive. She was dressed as coolly as possible while still looking professional, wearing a midthigh-length white skirt with a short white jacket over a modest V-neck blouse. She knew she stood out in the city, with her pale skin and hair and blue eyes. Although fluent in Spanish, it had taken her a week to realize the hissing was the Mexican form of wolf whistles. And the calls of *muy buenita* were not hard to figure out. Yet there'd been no time to explore the Latin lover mythos to see if there was any truth to it.

The train arrived; the same time, the same station, the same, every day. She could almost sleep on it except for having to be vigilant. As the doors sighed open Erica walked on, clutching her briefcase close. Her free hand reached toward the handhold as the doors shushed closed. Barely able to hang on in the crush of bodies that surrounded her, Erica divorced herself from the crowd and thought of lesson plans, almost as she had divorced herself from her marriage when George had stayed later and later at work until finally he didn't come home at all.

She always boarded the train at its fullest, with no place to sit, and she had a long stand to the end of the line. It was easy to fall into daydreaming and mulling over problems. Erica was so involved in thinking through a verb form issue that she almost didn't notice the hand that gently yet firmly gripped her right thigh. As if coming out of a dream, she felt the pressure first. She tried to move away, but there was no place to go, with bodies pressing in on her from all sides. She stared at the back of a man and could shift neither left nor right. Instead, she shifted her hips, but all that did was let the hand slide over and toward the inner curve of her thigh. Erica was surprised at the shiver that ran over her skin. One of her hands gripped the handhold; the other, her briefcase, and she could do nothing to stop a random stranger from touching her. The heat within built, and she melted a bit, as her body responded beyond her ability to control.

The train jerked as it came into a platform, and the hand slid a little higher, pushing up Erica's skirt. She closed her eyes, feeling the moisture gather between her legs. It had been so long since anyone had touched her. To be so desperate for a random stranger's touch shamed her, and her cheeks flushed. Yet her body responded in its own way.

In two more stops Erica would be getting off the train. She started now to push through the crowd, trying to turn about. The hand gave her a squeeze between the legs that brought a small gasp to her lips, and she turned. Looking up into the faces of the men around her, she could not tell who had touched her. They were staring off into nothing, reading papers, talking to each other or listening to music. Not one man looked guilty. No one glanced her way. There were at least four men standing near her. It could have been any one of them, but would she want to know the identity of the mystery man? What would she do? Accuse him and have everyone stare at her?

By the time her stop arrived, her fluttering heart had slowed and she exited the train, giving a small sway to her hips; a tease, in case the stranger watched her.

The next day, Erica didn't admit to herself that she dressed with a mind to the previous evening's incident. Her skirt was elegant, understated and midcalf length, with decorative buttons to just below the butt. Unfortunately, that day she was distracted enough that she spent too much time trying to write a proposal and now had more work to finish before the upcoming deadline.

The train was especially busy. Erica worked her way to a back corner where there was less chance of being smothered by pressing bodies, or of something being stolen. She managed to wedge in and then turned back to face the crowd so she could keep an eye on people. The intermittent air-conditioning on the train did little to alleviate the sweat trickling down her legs. Too many people and too hot a day. Erica wished she could melt, just to get away from the heat.

After four or five stops, Erica's mind wandered to the problems of her program. She'd stopped noticing the people coming and going until she felt a hand slide between her legs, halfway above her knees. Her body tensed as she felt the buttons being released. Obviously, he had already undone a few to get his hand in and she hadn't noticed. Then Erica changed; anticipation building in her, a thrum humming from her core, heating her in a way that blotted out the people around her. She stared ahead, seeing nothing as all attention centered on the hand working up her bare leg. The train jerked and fingers slid into the folds of her labia, burrowing through her already wet sex.

— 66 —

All she could do was close her eyes, taken away in the roar of her heart. Slowly, as the train trundled along, the hand wedged firmer between her folds, one finger moving forward and back, flicking over her clit. Erica's knees would have buckled had she not been wedged between so many people. The lights flickered off on the train and her mystery man took that moment to push two fingers up into her cunt. Erica moaned, her eyes closed. When she opened them, afraid of fainting, a man stared at her. She blushed, not having realized the lights had come back on. But the stranger's hand never stopped its slow movement within her.

She was so wet, and nearly quivering with pent-up lust. Could she come on the train without letting everyone know, with so many people around? Just as she thought she was going to have no choice and would have to just flow with the pleasure, she distinctly heard a voice whisper in Spanish, *"You have a hot little cunt."* The fingers quickly disappeared from between her legs, leaving her on the edge, shaking slightly.

Her heart thudded and she looked around, again unable to pinpoint who had touched her. She bit her lip. This was almost worse than no human touch at all; to be led to the brink and left hanging. By the time the train reached her stop, Erica had composed herself enough to walk off the train, albeit still thrumming inside. She realized that her skirt was undone to the last button just below her ass. Anyone watching would be seeing a good amount of leg, especially as she walked up the stairs.

By the time she entered her building, she nearly had to run into her apartment, before throwing herself down on the couch. Erica's fingers had barely rubbed over her clit before she came, and the heat flooded her, quaking her body with an orgasm that rippled over her. She lay there afterward, half on and half off the couch, drifting, feeling at once relaxed yet horny for the real thing. She wanted to be fucked, and the mystery man on the train had only awakened that burning need, making it tangible, harder to ignore. If only she weren't so busy. She sighed and sloughed off her clothes, throwing on shorts and a T-shirt as she pulled out papers to work on. It was only as she was hanging up her cotton jacket that she noticed a piece of paper in her pocket. All it gave was a time: 9:00 p.m. She smiled as heat touched her cheeks.

Perhaps she would be working late again.

In the morning, Erica put on a skirt she wouldn't normally wear to work. It was a green mini that came to just a few inches below her butt, with a large ruffle to it. Her blouse was light pink chiffon over a V-neck tank that accented her cleavage. She wore matching high wedge sandals, and draped a light sweater on her shoulders.

At the college, no one seemed to notice Erica's less than professional outfit, and since it was nearing end of term, many people worked late. When she left, she stuffed papers into an oversize bag, having foregone the briefcase, and then had to rush to catch the train. Her ride ran nearly from one end of the city to the other. It would have been a good night to drink some sangria. The heat lay about everyone like a thick blanket. And she was tired. The train was fairly empty at this time, with just enough people to occupy the seats. There was room to stand and move, so she made her way to her corner, away from the doors. Glancing that way, she saw three men, casually dressed and darkly handsome, standing there. They didn't act as if they knew each other and it was a common place to stand, out of the way.

Was one of them the man with the wandering hands?

One man was slim and tall and had the wavy brown hair and green eyes of mixed Spaniard blood. One was broad shouldered, with the hawk nose and deeper brown skin of an Aztec heritage, and the third man had black hair, sharp eyes, high cheekbones and was of a medium, almost nondescript build. If she had a choice, which would she choose?

Then the train began its long ride through the stifling heat of evening. If only it would rain, the humidity would go down. But Erica, for all the tension, still thought of lesson plans. Her hand kept slipping down the handhold from her sweat. As she gripped the bar a third time she felt two hands on her buttcheeks, squeezing, slowly crinkling up the short skirt. The temperature rose a few more degrees. And when had two men come to stand in front of her? She didn't remember anyone entering at the last few stops, but then she'd been thinking. Now all thoughts left her as the hands moved under the curve of each cheek and pulled.

She'd worn no underwear, and so was bare to the hands, and she could feel her lust dewing her. The fingers of one hand slid into her groove and flicked over her clit. Pressing her lips together, she tried hard not to moan out loud. Then she felt a firm rod of flesh press between her cheeks, and she couldn't help but gasp.

The two men in front of her blocked most of her view of the train, but when she looked around, she realized there were fewer passengers and no one was paying attention. Some had their eyes closed, some were reading. Then the lights flickered out and the man behind pushed Erica so that she had to hold her hands out or fall. Fall she did, toward someone in front. The person never turned in the darkness, never pushed her back.

She felt the cock push between her folds of flesh, sliding into her. A man was entering her on the train, the fat knob of his cock nosing in and gliding inside her.

The lights flickered back on, or so she thought, but the sensation grew so intense as he fucked her that she could not see clearly through the waves of heat that enveloped her, pouring out of her, down between her breasts and pooling in her core. He moved faster and faster, his cock building a friction of exquisite pleasure. Erica was terrified and exhilarated. Fucking on the train; would they get away with it? Could she stand the humiliation of being caught?

As the stranger behind her came, convulsing into her, he reached around and squeezed her nipples. She arched back, bearing down upon his cock, burrowing it as deep as it would go, and spasmed with the intensity. Opening her eyes, Erica noticed the lights had indeed come back on and the two men in front had turned to watch. They smiled knowingly.

Erica's cheeks burned. She was shocked at her own wanton behavior. She could excuse her need but she could not excuse her actions.

Then the one man watching, the tall Spanish-looking one with green eyes, moved very close to her and pushed her against the wall of the car. The other man had moved out from behind her and now stood in front, also blocking the view and keeping her cornered. The second one lifted her slightly, wedging between her legs, and almost before she knew it, he pushed into her, kissing her at the same time to keep her quiet.

He was large and slid slowly in. Erica moaned, moving the leg nearest the window up and around his waist. Once he was in all the way, he pulled back and then rammed her, slamming her into the wall. She clung on as he fucked her, the speed of the train equaling that of his pistoning cock. Her own juices trickled down her legs, her core melting with a mix of shame and lust and pure wanton fucking. Erica churned her hips, grinding back as she came, pulling the man over the edge with her. He groaned, the first sound she'd heard from him, as he pumped the last into her.

Then he stopped for a moment and withdrew. She heard one of the others say, "Our stop," and she realized the third would not do her, not today. But they all knew each other. It slowly dawned on her that this had been planned all along. She'd been led along, yet had she resisted?

The three men left at the next stop without looking back. Coolness whispered over her flesh for the first time in days, but somehow Erica knew that in the weeks to come the heat would build and there would be more than one way to ride the train.

ARIZONA, IRELAND, NEW ENGLAND

VERY YEAR, SUMMER COMES to the Arizona desert, although some say it never leaves. And summer comes to Ireland, although some say it never really arrives.

Jessamy emails Dara, a woman she's never met, although she knows her better than she knows her own sister. They met in an Internet chatroom, although both of them have forgotten which one. It's unimportant now. What matters is their friendship, and they exchange copious emails every day. They talk about important things: how to stretch their unemployment benefits; their neighbors, their infrequent middle-aged nights out; and whether Irish boxty is more like American grits or potato pancakes.

Dara tells Jessamy about the greenness and the quaintness of Ireland, painting a picture of a tranquil, rural life; where donkeys carry the turf to white-painted cottages, a story as appealing as it is inventive. And in return, Jessamy relates tales of coyotes, saguaro cacti reaching imploring arms to brilliant skies, and the merciless Arizona sun that shrivels all to bleached bones, a tale as fascinating as it is tall.

Dara sits in her tumbledown stone cottage in County Cork, which reeks of damp, and says wistfully, wouldn't it be a grand thing indeed if she could see the desert blooms for herself. She dreams of wide, white landscapes, and rattlesnakes in the laundry, and wakes in the morning with the smell of sage in her nostrils.

Jessamy slouches in her trailer on the edge of Tucson, wishing the landlord would repair the air-conditioning, and agrees. Dara would love the desert, and she, Jessamy, would love the curling turf and emerald wash of Ireland. She imagines a checked apron and herself carefully putting hens' eggs into the pockets.

A plan is made. They will swap houses for the summer, meeting when their flights connect in Boston, to hand over the keys, and again on the return trip to exchange tales.

They know each other instantly. The fuzzy scanned photos didn't do justice, of course, but they link arms like the bosom pals they are, and share a cab to the Holiday Inn. Two nights they have; two nights to see if their friendship translates into Real Life.

The friendship does more than merely translate, and on the first night one offers, the other accepts, and the air-conditioned room on the seventh floor turns into a trysting house. They explore, pressing and caressing flesh that is so familiar, yet eerily strange. Jessamy hovers, then delves between Dara's spread thighs and bites and laps, curling female moisture onto her tongue. Dara tastes of clover honey, she thinks fancifully, and dreams of lapping the cream from the top of a pint of Guinness.

Dara fingers and fondles, pistoning assertively into golden-pink yielding flesh, and curls her fingers around to seek the pleasure points. She compares the rush of moisture to the summer monsoons, which turn the arroyos into rushing torrents. She suckles at her lover's breast, and traces the suntan lines with her tongue. At the end of the summer she will be like this—a tawny creature, with long limbs of sun-gilded skin, and heat-streaked hair.

Jessamy compares her dark, dry hide to Dara's softer skin, clotted-cream pale. The gentle Irish summer will curl Jessamy's hair, soften it so that it hangs in springy curls on her shoulders. The temperate climate will be kind to her body, and she thinks of lazy days in a tiny bathroom with floral curtains at the windows, stroking lotion scented like tea roses into her skin. She runs gentle hands over her lover's flesh, feeling the slight catch as her rougher hands slide over skin as smooth as water.

Dara undulates up her lover's body to catch her lips in a kiss as fierce as the wind that curls along the desert pavement, whipping the sand into swirling eddies that beat against exposed tender flesh. Her tongue plunges deep, stabbing like cactus spines into flinching flesh. Dara's hands are firm, running in assertive patterns, pinching a nipple, biting on a yielding inner thigh so that the bruise blooms, cloudy, crushed-purple marks of possession.

Jessamy yields, her body melting bonelessly into the bed, soft, springy like the sodden tea-colored turf, as she raises a leg and clasps Dara so that her head is encompassed between her fleshy thighs. Dara's mouth can now flicker with glorious friction on Jessamy's sex, so that the orgasm builds, slowly, wetly, until it breaks in a sun-gold crimson tide, sweeping her away from the Holiday Inn.

In a fluid motion, their positions change, and Jessamy pushes and rubs with a deliberate finger frottage, exploring through folds and damp crevices. She insinuates her way so slowly, stimulating so gently that Dara is not aware of the rising climax until it seeps over her, washing from fingers to toes, swelling outward from her sex in deep, dark pulses.

Their sleep is disturbed by dreams, fractured images of waking dreams to come. Dara dreams of how the light will fall clear and sharp over the Sonoran Desert. How she will fearlessly sweep a scorpion from the kitchen bench with a swift flick of a tea towel. Jessamy falls into dreams of drowning; black tea pools of bog land, hazy in the twilight, blurred by the soft rain. Herself, sipping on a pint, playing the fiddle with men in tweed caps, her foot tapping the rhythm.

By day, the women explore Boston. Jessamy buys a porcelain coyote figurine, a bandana around its neck, head raised and howling. She will stand it on Dara's bathroom window ledge, next to the red-haired girl in a step-dancing costume that she knows is there, and it will remind her of what she's left. In an Irish shop, Dara buys a St. Brigid's cross, woven not of reeds but shaped in clay. She will hang it above the doorway of Jessamy's trailer, above the Navajo rug on the floor, and it will be a small image of home in an alien landscape.

That night, they return to the Holiday Inn and they return to each other, falling onto the bed with indecent haste, shedding clothes, baring flesh to latch on to a nipple, part pale or golden thighs and dive between. The Holiday Inn is insulated from the real world outside; the summer can't penetrate its walls and the air-conditioning negates any trace of heat or humidity. But to Dara, the room and her lover are as exotic as the surreal cacti that she'll see tomorrow. The sharp taste of

Jessamy's cunt is as unusual as the *nopales* and scrambled eggs she'll eat for her first Arizona breakfast. Taking the razor she uses to shave her underarms, she scrapes her lover's pussy bare so that the folds stand out in stark relief. A paradox; bare abraded flesh outside, but inside, secret moist places, slick as summer rain.

Jessamy considers the razor but sets it aside. She tangles her fingers in Dara's abundant thatch of turf-dark pubic hair, parting sodden curls to find the drowned, wet depths they guard. To her, this room is secret and dark, and the things they do here will be forever held close to her heart, as mysterious and strange as the holy shrine where she'll light a candle tomorrow.

That night, neither of them dreams.

Every morning, Dara opens the door of Jessamy's trailer, sketches the sign of the cross, gives a quick flicker of acknowledgment to the St. Brigid's cross above the door, and sits down on the step with a cup of tea. She stares at the desert and shudders as a centipede runs across her foot. Then she goes into the small kitchen to cook what passes for bacon here, throwing the scraps into open bins, which will be raided by scavenging coyotes. Later, in bed, Dara will shiver under the thin sheet, as she listens to their snarls, and prays that they don't attack her.

Jessamy shivers, stepping into the damp bathroom. Every day, the mold creeps further across the ceiling, an advancing olive bloom. She bemoans the absence of real coffee, and sits inside at the kitchen table, watching the rain stream down the small panes. Turning the heating up another notch, she contemplates a visit to the village shop, where, once again, she will not understand a word of the thick local accents.

Later, she will go to the pub and stare into a pint of Guinness, trying to convince herself she likes the taste.

Both women dream of two nights to come in New England.

Saskia Walker

THE THINGS THAT GO ON AT SIESTA TIME

E VERYTHING WAS QUIET. It was midafternoon, siesta time. The sun smoldered across the crystalline-blue sky over Crete, sparkling off the Aegean Sea and making every rock, wall and tile glow. Nikoleta shielded her eyes and stepped quickly over the sun-baked rocks that led up to the back of the villa. She kicked off her sandals, stepped out of her uniform and sat down, resting her back against the shady wall behind her. The heat didn't bother Nikoleta, but the companion she was expecting was fair-skinned and needed the shade. Lydia. Lydia with the long legs and the big, baby blue eyes. Nikoleta's mouth watered just thinking about her.

There were so many advantages to working for the big-shot English movie producer. She got paid very well indeed, more than any maid in her village—a secluded backwash on the island, far from the tourist resorts where good jobs were more plentiful. The family was only going to be in the villa for a few months of the year, but intended to pay the staff all year round. The villagers were always eager for the gossip about who came and went at the big house and—best of all— she had access to the lovely Lydia, the daughter of the house.

Lydia had turned nineteen that year. She was fair and lithe; spoilt and incredibly naive. She pouted and preened, wandering around the grounds of the villa half-undressed, exposing herself in skimpy bikinis, shorts that frayed up over the cheeks of her cute behind and halter-necked tops that revealed the outline of her pert little breasts. Every man in the village lusted after the pretty English girl and a chorus of whistles followed her whenever she rode her bicycle around the local area. Lydia clearly loved that kind of attention, but Nikoleta didn't think the little madam was helping herself any. Nikoleta was a very practical woman. She could see it made Lydia even hotter; her chaotic sexual chemistry swamped the entire household.

Nikoleta had watched as Lydia flirted outrageously with Stefanos and Alec, the groundsmen. She lay on her sun lounger by the pool rubbing lotion into her bare limbs, flicking through trashy romance novels looking for the dirty parts. She'd pause and slip her shades down to inspect the men while they fished leaves out of the pool, eyeing their sleek muscled bodies at work. Those poor men were in a constant state of arousal with that little sex bomb on hand—so near, and yet so far out of their reach. Nikoleta smiled to herself and smugly treasured the fact that she'd gotten the first taste of the lovely Lydia that sultry summer.

She had discovered quite by chance that Lydia responded to both idle caresses and outright groping. She brushed out her long blonde hair in the mornings and touched the soft skin of her neck and shoulders, stroking the flaxen strands down over her chest. Lydia gasped and whimpered, but didn't tell the maid to stop. Nikoleta murmured compliments, purring constantly and growling at the back of her throat whenever she made eye contact. When she helped her choose what to wear from the long walk-in wardrobe stuffed with clothes, Nikoleta got even bolder. She held things up against Lydia with cheeky hands, hands that molded the material in against her breasts and over her hips, both dextrous and suggestive. Lydia's body was programmed to respond. Riddled with frustration, she leached against the wily maid for more contact, staring at Nikoleta with wide eyes and open lips, whimpering, her breath constricted, while Nikoleta fondled her body through the skimpiest of barriers. Nikoleta knew Lydia could only hold out so long. She was a sexual time bomb that was about to blow. Nikoleta grinned; she was getting nearer her target. She kept up that intrusive routine until there was such a plea in Lydia's eyes that it was obvious she had reached the point of desperation.

"Nikoleta…" she declared. "You are touching me like a man would!"

"Oh, but you like it, yes," Nikoleta chuckled. Lydia's cheeks burned but she seemed unable to deny it. Nikoleta took her chance.

"Take off your robe," she whispered. "I am here to help you." Lydia obeyed. When she was naked, Nikoleta dropped the dress she had held out in one hand and pushed Lydia back into the darkest recess of the wardrobe.

"You're so hot," she declared, squeezing Lydia's peaked nipples.

"That feels so good," she murmured, her body trembling with need. Nikoleta kissed her mouth to quiet the desperate moans of pleasure while she plundered Lydia's intimate flesh with knowing fingers. She had responded like a forest fire suddenly blazing out of control; hot, wild, desperate and clambering all over Nikoleta, even more responsive and willing than Nikoleta had guessed she might be, bucking wildly and crying at the point of her climax.

High with the thrill of dominating the English girl and wet with wanting herself, Nikoleta stepped back, hoisted her skirt, squeezed her pussy lips hard, and then rubbed and flicked her clit, quickly, while Lydia stared at her lusty new lover with fascinated eyes. When she ventured to touch Nikoleta's sex, Lydia soon found her fingers crushed and her hand completely drenched. From that point on the two young women ricocheted together in an almost constant cycle of arousal and fulfillment, each day bringing new games and pleasures. These were new games for Lydia, but she was well and truly hooked.

This was their third time meeting outside. The spot was perfect; they were outside basking in the warm breeze and yet they were so secluded. The large flat rocks bedded in against the villa wall were overhung with honeysuckle and bougainvillea, shady and intoxicating. Nikoleta brushed the falling blossoms off her shoulder and pulled off her bra, her nipples growing hard and tingling at the sight of Lydia's lithe body hurrying over. She drew to a giddy halt, wisps of fair hair escaping from her ponytail, her aquamarine sarong wavering gently around her legs. She was breathless and flushed with arousal.

"Let me see you," Nikoleta whispered, lifting the hem of Lydia's sarong. She snaked one hand up around the calf of her leg, looking up at her from below. Lydia gasped and laughed, glancing over her shoulder back along the path behind her. She was still worried about discovery, but Nikoleta—being practical— reminded her it was siesta time. Besides which, Nikoleta's dark suggestions had an almost hypnotic effect on Lydia; she had no choice but to submit. She lifted the sarong, slowly revealing the curves of her inner thighs. Nikoleta watched with blatant, hungry eyes.

She was naked beneath, wearing just the bikini top and sarong. The mound at the juncture of Lydia's thighs was so softly rounded and firm that Nikoleta's mouth ached to bite the flesh and stick her tongue into the dewy niche.

"You are so wet, so ready...."

Lydia nodded vigorously. "I was getting so bloody horny, waiting in my room...." She untied the bikini top. Her breasts jutted forward, nipples the color of wine against the pale marble of her skin. Nikoleta pulled her down onto the flat rock, rolling over and quickly pinning her. Lydia's head rolled from side to side, her legs opening.

"Hurry, before someone sees us," she declared, her eyes pleading with Nikoleta to be quick. Nikoleta smiled. She never rushed. The threat of being discovered would keep Lydia trembling on the point of climax, while Nikoleta gave her sweet torture with strokes of her tongue, mouth and fingers. Lydia shuddered and moaned, her lean body prone in submission.

"Everyone is asleep...." She rose up, pinning her friend down with her hands on her shoulders, and looked at her body with hungry eyes.

"For God's sake, Nikoleta, do me...." she begged.

Chuckling, Nikoleta lowered her head to trail her tongue over the girl's belly and lower, warm breath moving the fair hair at her groin, the tip of her wet tongue parting the intimate folds. The inflamed morsel of her clit reared up between the plump, swollen folds of skin. She sucked then tongued the sensitive nub, stroking further down each time and sticking her tongue into the tight core of Lydia's sex. She sighed. She was in heaven there. Then a draft came up from somewhere and wafted the scent of flowers over them. Lydia's body grew still. A shadow had fallen over them. Nikoleta lifted her head. Lydia's expression was horror-struck as she stared over Nikoleta's shoulders.

"Oh fuck it, I'm dead," she uttered, eyes closing.

Nikoleta turned. Stefanos was standing behind them. His eyes were glazed, and he had a leering smile on his face. Nikoleta's eyes dropped to his belt. His shorts were stretched tight over his crotch, a huge erection threatening to rip the fabric asunder. He'd been watching them and he'd gotten turned on. It served him right. Stefanos was a dirty spy. Why, just that morning she had spotted him watching her while she was doing her sweeping. He had stood on a box and peered over the edge of the terrace to look up at her from below. Nikoleta knew full well he was watching, but instead of shooing him off she bent over her task and hitched her skirt up around her hips, giving him a look at everything he was missing. Nikoleta never wore knickers. That was his punishment.

"Don't worry," she whispered. "He is coming here to us, not going into the house to tell…." She soothed her friend, stroking her long hair back from her face. Then she spoke to him in Greek; he didn't speak any English. Stefanos laughed and nodded at her words, his thick black hair falling forward as he did so. "He wants, how do you say it, a piece of your action?" She nodded down toward the tumescent bulge below his belted waist.

"He wants me?" Lydia whispered, through fingers that covered her mouth and quelled her rapid breathing while she stared at the handsome boy. Nikoleta reached over and pulled Lydia's hand away from her face, kissing her gently on the cheek. She whispered in her ear.

"Yes, he wants you. Do you want to try him now? You've had one before, right? A man?"

"Well, yes, once, and to be honest it was pretty crap, but...the bloke didn't look anything like it...I mean him." Nikoleta patted her bottom approvingly. Stefanos was watching them, eagerly awaiting their reaction to his obvious intentions.

"You like it, yes?" Nikoleta chuckled. Lydia was staring, while she worked her thighs together, crushing her pussy lips. She nodded vaguely. "Okay, I will tell him you want it and he can fuck you now." Remember, Nikoleta was a very practical sort. Lydia grew serious as she committed herself. She nodded again, eagerly.

Nikoleta asked him to show himself. She was having fun. She wanted to see Lydia with that big cock inside her. Stefanos was eager, too. He unbelted his shorts before she finished the instruction to do so, dropping them to the ground and kicking them to one side, revealing the stout, long bough of his erect cock. He was huge and laden, his balls hanging heavily against his thighs. His cock twitched when both women stared at it. Nikoleta beckoned to him with her hand, pointing down to the largest flattish rock, the one where they had been lying together.

Nikoleta glanced at Lydia, whose eyebrows lifted in question. "He is ours." Nikoleta's eyes glittered with pleasure. She snatched at Lydia's hand, drawing her in. "You are ready?" Lydia nodded. His cock twitched again, its surface sheened and silken. "Climb onto him, as you would your bicycle, that way I can watch better." Stefanos moaned loudly when he realized they were negotiating positions. Nikoleta felt a pang of pity for him; he was quite obviously desperate for release and the horny action he'd been watching earlier had only made his problem that much bigger. His shaft was huge. Lydia hunched down beside him, then lifted one knee over his hips, coming to rest with her sex just above the broad head of his cock. She looked around at Nikoleta.

"Christ, Nikoleta, help me, it's so bloody big," she whispered. Nikoleta beamed; to have the two of them so needy of her assistance was quite delicious in itself. Then, as she knelt down beside them, she felt Stefanos touching her hip. She looked down as his fingers reached for her pussy. He asked her to sit on his face. Her smile grew wide and her eyes flashed with greedy anticipation. She straddled his head, facing Lydia. She lowered herself slowly onto his open mouth and began working herself against him, slowly at first, then more urgently.

Lydia watched, eyes wide. When Nikoleta had found her rhythm she leaned forward and moved his erect cock toward the entrance of Lydia's plump, damp channel. The crown of his cock was so large that she had to ease it in very slowly, working the juices that oozed down against its hardness, to help its passage. Lydia whimpered; her body flexed and became taut, then her head went back in ecstasy, her hips moving forward to embrace the hard thing more vigorously when her body learned its measure. Nikoleta felt Stefanos stirring under her, responding to the twin pleasures. His mouth grew more anxious on her intimate flesh, his tongue probing into her channel, strong and long, bringing on more liquid heat from inside her.

"Oh, my, it's so large," Lydia stuttered, gasping.

Nikoleta gave a throaty chuckle. "Press down, it will not harm you, precious one; enjoy him."

Lydia's eyes closed and Nikoleta watched her riding the rigid column of flesh. A perverse sense of pleasure traveled through her as she watched and felt all at once. Lydia looked almost ready to collapse with pleasure and she began to plunge faster. Nikoleta suddenly felt a pang of envy; the crown of that magnificent cock must feel so good, buried in deep. She could see each exquisite spasm reflected in the expression on Lydia's face. Then, suddenly, she felt Stefanos buffeting her pussy lips more vigorously, thrusting his tongue faster, teeth nipping at her clit as he began to buck beneath her. Lydia let out a yowl of extreme pleasure, her body shuddering with release.

His body was taut with submission. Even if she hadn't known that he was coming by the way his face moved distractedly against her flesh, she saw it ride up in Lydia's body—the renewed tenseness in her hips, her mouth a delectable open circle, a low moan in her throat. She wrapped her slender arms around herself and rocked on him, as if savoring the feeling.

A few moments later both women hauled themselves up and looked down at him. His breath was ragged. He was distracted, his expression vague, his eyes barely open. Nikoleta smiled.

"Look, his cock is beautiful, let's enjoy him for as long as we can," Nikoleta said, her voice a whisper, the pounding inside her core barely relenting. Lydia nodded, transfixed by the stretch of strong male flesh. They moved to either side of him. Nikoleta kissed his face, licking her cream from his cheeks. He was strong and smelt good, like he'd been helping himself to the master's cologne. Lydia fondled his thighs, while Nikoleta's curious hands roved over his chest and slid down the line of dark hair that guided her to the plumage that sprang in his groin. Her fingers settled there and stirred. He moaned in delight, undeniably pinned by their dextrous fingers on his body.

She looked down at his cock. It was beginning to become erect again. There was only one thing a practical woman could do. She reached for it, stroking it as it began to grow quicker in her hand. The power of it growing beneath her fingers affected her. She preferred playing with women, but she suddenly felt rampant and wild with this thing in her hand. Her pussy ached for it. The shaft was rigid now, hot, and ready. She wanted to feel its strength inside her body, just as Lydia had. She bent down and kissed its swollen tip and then tasted his essence with her tongue, sweeping over the firm, soft surface in circular movements. A thread of urgency flew round her blood, she was desperate: he was more than ready to be mounted again. She climbed onto him and when she had taken him to the hilt she groaned. It felt so very good, she could hardly move. Then she began riding him, hard and fast. She was close to flooding.

His chest arched up toward her, his rib cage jutting, his neck a line of tensed muscle. His eyes begged her for his second release. The swell and throb of his pulsating rod was so insistent, her flesh began to melt and shift around it. His fingers fumbled where he entered her body, stroking at the point where their flesh met, the cup of his hand latched over her swollen clit. Nikoleta was impressed. Her pussy clutched at him, rhythmic and intense, then spasmed. She bit her lip to stop herself from screaming aloud. His eyebrows drew down and Nikoleta felt the line of muscle that stretched from his hip down the front of his thighs tighten and reach beneath her. Her body was lifted up with its strength. When he came it was with mighty, Herculean lunges.

The end of siesta time was near.

The three revelers dressed quickly. Nikoleta smiled, like a cat with all the cream. She'd sampled the goods and enjoyed them. She told Stefanos that if he kept quiet he could come back for more. With him involved, their games were going to be even better: the possibilities were endless.

"Are you sure he's not going to tell anyone?" Lydia asked.

"He will keep the secret so that he can have some more now and next summer…when you come back to us." She smiled at Lydia. "Also, I can think of at least one way to keep him quiet, in between." She turned to Stefanos and winked. He grinned back at her. She had decided that she liked him, after all, and—being a practical sort—she knew she would need something to keep her warm through the long winter months ahead.

LISABET SARAI

MaD DOGS

VENTUALLY, I'LL WRITE ABOUT THIS. The cracked, grimy ceiling that's there whenever I open my eyes. The raspy hiccuping of the fan. The momentary relief when it swings in my direction; air hot against my naked, eternally sweaty skin, but moving at least. The scents of frying garlic and rotting fish and stagnant water, the singsong voices of the vendors under my window, the quavering pop music and the honking of the taxis on New Road.

Exotic Thailand. I'll capture it all, the mysterious complexity and the gritty foreignness. A brilliant cross between E. M. Forster and Jack Kerouac: young man adrift, living on the fringe, self-abandoned in a strange land, victim of bad judgment and bad luck. A suitable subject for a talented writer like myself, full of irony and pathos.

Right now, though, my head aches. Even indoors, with the stained cotton drapes half-closed, the heat is a hammer, mashing my fine mind to incoherent pulp. I lie here paralyzed, arms and legs spread wide on the hard mattress to increase the surface area exposed to the limping fan. I lie here, as I do every day, waiting for the sun to sink low enough to make walking on the baked sidewalks tolerable.

Usually about five o'clock I manage to rouse myself, throw on a T-shirt and shorts, and do my daily business. My pilgrimage to the main post office, only a block away, my daily penance at the Poste Restante counter, the pitying smile from the plump clerk as she shakes her head yet again.

No, sir, no mail for Michaelson today. Sorry.

It's already mid-April. When I spoke to her last month, Marcia told me she expected a response by the end of March. But publishers are unpredictable, and agents are notoriously busy. I can't afford to call her often, but I guess I'll have to try again Monday night (Monday morning in New York), try to catch her before her week is completely booked and shame her into badgering New American Library yet again. I'm no longer Marcia's top priority. Out of sight, out of mind.

Thailand. It had seemed like such an inspired notion when René proposed it to me over our beers last January. René was buying. I had just been laid off holiday duty from Barnes and Noble.

The gutters overflowed with gray slush. The pitiless wind whistled through the city's artificial canyons.

"I can't afford to live in the city," I complained. "But where can I go? Back to Illinois? That would be career suicide. No serious author ever came from Peoria!"

"Why don't you take a sabbatical?"

"Sabbatical? I can't pay my rent!"

"Sublet your place, take whatever money you can scrape up, and go to Thailand. Beautiful girls. Glittering temples. Fabulous, spicy food. No snow. It's incredibly cheap, if you know the right places. Phone and Internet are just as good as here. You can relax, have a good time, maybe do some writing, while you wait for the news about your novel."

Beautiful girls. Now that sounded appealing. Since Lisa had dumped me, just before Thanksgiving, my romantic landscape had been as bleak as the city streets.

I didn't miss Lisa, not exactly. But jacking off is a supremely lonely activity.

So the picture René painted of high-spirited, hedonistic Bangkok sounded like the ideal answer. Especially when he volunteered to join me for a week or two.

I cashed the savings bond that had been my parents' graduation gift to me. I found a fairly reliable acquaintance whose boyfriend had just thrown him out to take over my apartment. I had a fifteen-minute meeting with Marcia in which she promised to keep the pressure on NAL. I sent a letter to my mom and dad, vaguely suggesting that I had a writing assignment overseas. Once I made the decision, everything seemed to flow smoothly.

Now, two months later, I'm stuck here, mired in the gooey underbelly of Bangkok like a dinosaur in a tar pit. Money almost gone. Nothing left but my return ticket, my laptop, and my dubious genius. Sure, I could limp back home, a whipped dog with my tail between my legs. Back to what, though? Working with Dad in the hardware store?

I accept the inevitable. Dragging myself out of bed, I put on the minimum acceptable amount of clothing. The loose cotton shirt clings to my damp back. The zipper of my fly grates uncomfortably against my flaccid cock, but the notion of underwear is simply unbearable.

I pull my laptop out of its hiding place behind the scarred bureau. Tool of my trade. I've hardly opened it since I got here. I stuff the computer in a shopping bag and head for the street.

It's well past three. I weave my way along the fractured pavement, trying to stay in the shade. Whenever I fail, the fierce sun pummels me, pounding my skull despite my hat. A couple of bareheaded, red-faced tourists stroll past me, wearing cheap batik and gold jewelry. What's that saying about mad dogs and Englishmen?

I spend three quarters of an hour breathing exhaust on the open bus before I get to Pantip Plaza. The used computer places are on the third floor. I ride up the escalators, rock music and video game sound effects blaring from every shop. I catch the scents of Chinese incense and fried chilis.

When I find the stall I'm looking for, the transaction takes no more than ten minutes. I do my best to haggle, but the shopkeeper recognizes my aura of desperation. I stuff the wad of thousand-baht notes in my pocket, sending one last regretful look back at my friendly Toshiba. The skinny young man already has it disassembled on his table.

Feeling flush, I splurge on a taxi back. Rush hour makes it a long, slow ride, but in the sterile chill of the air-conditioning, I hardly mind. I close my eyes and lean back. The throbbing in my temples gradually dies away.

It won't be in vain, I resolve. Who needs a computer? Did Hemingway have a computer? I'll pick up a notebook tomorrow, and from now on, I'll spend at least three hours a day working. What else have I got to do, after all?

The irrational pattern of one-way streets means that the taxi has to let me off a couple of blocks from the guesthouse. That's okay, though. The sun has sunk below the horizon by now. There's even a hint of breeze coming from the river, stirring the muggy air.

I'm revived by the air-conditioning and my fresh resolution. I stride down the sidewalk, maneuvering around the other pedestrians, avoiding the cracked bricks and crumbling curbs almost by instinct. Maybe coming to Bangkok *was* a good idea. After all, there's that old wisdom about having to hit bottom before you start to recover.

His body slams into me without warning. As I stumble and fall to my knees, I have a confused impression of tight jeans, flashy jewelry, silky black hair. Sandalwood cologne.

"Oh, I'm sorry, sir! Are you okay?" He helps me up, brushing the dust off my pants. "Please forgive me! I'm so clumsy." His voice is soft and musical, with the pleasing cadence of Thai-accented English.

"It's all right. Never mind," I tell him. His arched eyebrows are drawn together in a concerned frown, but a smile hovers on his full lips. *"Mai pen rai."*

"Are you sure? Can I help you to your hotel?" I'm suddenly aware of his manicured hand resting on my shoulder, light as a butterfly. His exotic scent makes me slightly dizzy. I look him over. His designer shirt, in muted stripes, fits his slender torso and broader shoulders like a second skin. His stretch denim trousers look painted on. He has gold rings on every finger, and one in his left earlobe.

He's a creature of beauty. I'm suddenly ashamed of myself, sweaty and unkempt, with two days' beard. I don't want him to see the dingy hole where I live.

"No, thanks, that's not necessary. It's not your fault. The sidewalks here are treacherous. It's easy to lose your balance."

"Okay, then. See you."

He saunters away, graceful despite the hazards of the broken pavement. I watch him for a moment. There's an odd tightness in my chest, and I still feel a bit woozy. Too much sun, I think, turning back toward my destination. I should know better than to come out during the day. At least I accomplished my goal, though. I pat my pocket, seeking reassurance in the fat mass of folded bills stashed there.

And feel nothing.

My pocket is empty. It takes several seconds before I understand. Then I let out a howl that sends both tourists and natives scattering in alarm.

"NO! No, damn it! You bastard!" I turn back in the direction I came from, trying to run, stumbling and cursing my own stupidity. The slick young thief has disappeared, of course. Before long, I'm gasping from the heat and pollution. Pain lances through my forehead. Black spots dance in front of my eyes.

I sink down onto the step of a shuttered shop, barely able to breathe. Despair washes over me. It's all over. No money, no computer, no future. I might as well be dead. Tears of frustration and self-pity spill down onto my shirt, already muddy with dust and sweat. I squeeze my eyes shut, willing the darkness inside my soul to take over my consciousness.

I smell him before I see him. "Hey, you." The voice is gentle, almost sad. "Don't cry. Never mind. Here." A folded wad of paper is pushed into my hand. "Take it."

Incredulous, I open my eyes. He's crouched beside me, thighs spread wide for balance. His hand is on my shoulder once again. He pulls a silk handkerchief from the pocket of his jeans. It's still warm from his body.

I look down at the beige banknotes in my palm. "It's all there," he says. "You can count it if you want."

"Why…?"

He shrugs. "I like you," he says, his half smile widening to a grin.

I notice a tourist police kiosk across the street, its occupant watching us curiously. I stuff the money deep into my pocket. I don't care whether or not he's telling the truth.

"Hey, you want a beer? My friends have a place down the next *soi*." He rises from his haunches with a dancer's grace and holds out his hand to help me up. "My name is Bom. And you?"

"Gary." I'm still suspicious, not sure I should trust him.

"Come on, Gary." He throws his arm around my shoulders and leads me away. In the brooding heat of dusk, I expect to find his touch unpleasant, but it's strangely comforting. I guess I'm not over the shock of my near-disaster.

His silk shirt slithers against the bare skin on my arms. I worry about the dirt on my own clothes, but Bom doesn't seem to care.

He leads me down a lane that dead-ends at the river. A dilapidated wooden shack on stilts perches precariously over the muddy water. The door's wide open; inside I see several young men gathered round a table, and an inviting-looking plastic tub filled with ice and bottles of Singha.

Bom introduces his friends. Their monosyllabic names go in one ear and out the other. They're all dressed like Bom, skintight jeans and tailored silk shirts, accented by gold amulets and fancy watches.

Bom hands me an open beer. The chilled amber liquid slides down my throat, a sensual delight. He tips his head back to take a swig from his own bottle. My eyes are drawn to the elegant curve of his neck. He wears his hair long, in a ponytail down his back. A lock has come loose and hangs in his eyes, giving him a waifish look.

His friends are laughing and chattering in Thai. The polite host, Bom tries to make conversation. "Are you here on holiday?"

"I'm a writer." This doesn't really answer the question, but he nods as if satisfied. "I'm working on a novel."

"About Thailand?"

"Partly."

"Ooh! Maybe you'll put me in it." He grins with almost childish delight.

I take refuge in silence, taking another swallow of my beer. I'm surprised to find the bottle is already empty. Before I can even ask, Bom hands me a full one. I drink deeply, gazing out the open window at the twilight river traffic.

The barges make their stately way upstream, ponderous and silent. Swarms of long tail powerboats zip around them, buzzing like insects. A tourist dinner cruise sweeps by, a floating Christmas tree outlined in tiny flashing lights. I'm feeling quite drunk, and oddly peaceful. I let everything flow by me.

The place reeks of fish and rusted iron. Under these raw smells, I catch a whiff of Bom's sandalwood cologne. He has lapsed into Thai with his cohorts, abandoning any attempts to communicate with me. Still, he makes sure that the bottle in front of me is always full.

Overwhelmed by the beer and the day's events, I fall asleep. Sometime later I wake, disoriented, in near-darkness. A halogen lamp mounted on the next pier sends uneven shafts of light into the shack, but until my eyes adjust, I can barely see anything.

The chairs clustered around the Formica-topped table are all empty. The table itself is littered with dozens of empty bottles. The room is quiet enough that I can hear the river lapping against the piles that support the building.

Then I recognize the sound of breathing. As this is sinking in, somebody moans.

"Bom?" There's a creaking sound off in the corner.

"Here, Gary." His voice is muffled. Someone bursts into laughter, which breaks off suddenly to become a groan of pleasure.

I'm beginning to make out my surroundings. There's some kind of platform at the far end of the room. The platform is covered with pale, writhing, naked bodies.

"Come on, Gary," Bom coaxes. He is on his knees, poised above the prone body of one of his friends. Even in the dimness, I can see the gleam of his perfect skin, the smile on his ripe lips. He bends once more to the cock jutting up in front of him.

Another of his mates is positioned behind Bom's hips. He grabs Bom's buttocks, pulls them open, and begins lapping at his friend's anus.

My cock hardens rapidly. If I were sober, I'd probably find this alarming, but at the moment, it seems completely normal. I unsnap, unzip, and wrestle my cock into the open air. It swells further, grateful to be set free. I stroke it slowly, root to tip, my attention fixed on the scene in front of me.

For a while the action is languid, dreamy; slow-motion caresses are punctuated every now and then by a sharp intake of breath or a sudden groan. My cock surges in my hand in reaction. I can hear the slurp of tongues against wet flesh, but it's a bit difficult to see the details.

Hardly realizing what I'm doing, I move closer, still stroking myself. The guy with his face buried in Bom's ass sits back on his haunches. He looks over at me and grins as he rolls a condom over his impressive prick. He says something in Thai. Bom hikes his rear up higher. He wiggles his butt in invitation.

The other man positions the tip of his rod between Bom's asscheeks. He jerks his hips, and his cock disappears from view. Bom wails as though in pain. His partner pulls back, then rams his cock back into Bom, raising another yell from my Thai friend.

I can't really see what's going on, but I can guess. My own asshole twitches in sympathy. My cock jumps with every thrust. I remember vividly the one time I had anal sex with Lisa, the way her hole gripped my cock when I plunged into her, the way her flesh gaped and shuddered whenever I pulled out. I remember her roaring orgasm, and her tears afterward. She wouldn't let me do it again, and she flatly refused to stick even one finger up my ass.

I can't imagine what it would feel like to have that huge, rigid prick boring into my butt. Just thinking about it, though, brings me close to the edge.

The action's rougher now, and louder too. Another couple is fucking, between Bom and the shed wall. The one's who's taking it is on his back, bent double, his legs practically by his ears. His partner straddles him, drilling into him from above. My eyes are better adjusted to the dimness now. I can see the corded muscles of the fucker's thighs and the sweat dripping down his back as he pistons in and out of the other man's hole.

There's a fifth guy, the one that Bom had been sucking. He's still on his back underneath Bom, jerking off energetically in time to the cock pounding Bom's bowels. Just as I notice him, he screams and lets go, showering Bom's face with thick white droplets.

I'm almost there myself. The ache in my balls is unbearable. I jerk and pull on myself, faster, harder, close but somehow unable to get over the edge.

"Gary," Bom says hoarsely, rising up onto his knees. "Closer. Please." His partner has paused, cock still buried in Bom's hole. I move to the side of the platform, squeezing my aching prick.

Bom puts his arm around my neck and pulls my face to his. He tastes of stale beer and bitter semen. He smells of sweat. His tongue coils inside my mouth, exploring the possibilities. It's muscular and playful and this is not at all like kissing Lisa.

I kiss him back, rubbing my swollen prick against his naked, come-smeared belly. Nothing has ever felt so good.

Bom smiles when he feels my cock poking at him. He grabs it, pushing my own hands away, and laughs softly, then pulls my pants down around my knees. "Very nice. Oh yes, I like it. Can I have it?"

He doesn't wait for permission. Bending back down, he sucks my cock into his eager mouth. Sensation overwhelms me. Sultry jungle heat swallows me up. His tongue sweeps up and down, massaging, teasing. I want more and so I take it, ramming my cock down his throat. The bulb mashes against his palate. He gags, then opens wider, taking my whole length. The next moment he's using his teeth, nipping at the ridge under the head. I roar and slam my prick back where it belongs, as deep into him as I can go.

All at once, his body shakes with a new rhythm. He's being fucked again, I realize. He moans around my cock. I fuck his mouth while his friend fucks his ass, thrust for thrust.

I'm ready to explode; the guy reaming Bom yells and shudders. He pounds his hips convulsively against Bom's buttcheeks. I know he's pouring his come into Bom's hole. The image brings me right to the edge.

Bom writhes, but doesn't let up on the suction. I feel hot jets of viscous stuff landing on my bare thighs. Bom is coming all over me.

I can't take any more. I swell and explode into Bom's mouth. He swallows, sucks, swallows again. The pleasure is outrageous. I'm totally lost in the sensations. My cock is starting to deflate, yet still I shudder and jerk like a puppet. Finally, my cock slips limply from between the Thai man's lips. He's smiling. A Buddha image hangs on his hairless chest, between tender-looking nipples.

I'll be damned if I don't start to get hard again.

Without saying a word, Bom turns his back to me and presents his ass. Dripping down the cleft between those two pale moons, I see a trail of wetness.

I can't help myself. My forefinger reaches out, tracing the path of the other man's come downward until I brush my fingertip over the velvety skin of Bom's scrotum. He sighs with delight. Fascinated, I slide my finger back up through the crevice, and sink it into that slick, dark orifice that beckons irresistibly.   ·

He tightens around the invading digit; I slip in a second finger next to the first.

Somebody hands me a condom.

I'll write about this someday, this crazy night outside of time. The boats chugging past in the distance, the scent of rust and garbage, the mournful folk song filtering in on the tropical breeze. The alcohol-induced haze that makes everything beautiful and unreal.

Right now, though, all I want is to fuck this gorgeous, seductive, treacherous creature until we're both senseless.

TERESA NOELLE ROBERTS

LEARNING HIS ROPES

LEANOR WOKE IN THE HOTEL ROOM to the sound of waves, still feeling boneless and content, not to mention still a little sticky and sore in interesting places from their earlier play. Nick woke when she got up, blew her a kiss, then sprawled catlike to take over the spot she'd vacated in the king-sized bed. She grabbed his big T-shirt off the floor—her own clothes looked like too much work and the shirt was almost as long as her skirt anyway—popped it over her head, and wandered out onto the balcony.

The thunderstorm that had driven them off the beach had come and gone, leaving a cool, misty evening in its wake, wrapping the ocean below them in a light fog. She hadn't thought Ogunquit Beach could look prettier than it had at sunrise, or under the threat of glowering thunderheads with the sea like angry steel, but the fog gave it a romantic air that made it even more inviting. The cooler air made Eleanor's nipples pucker, raised goose bumps on her skin.

So did the feel of Nick's body, pressing unexpectedly up against her from behind, his arms cupping her breasts. Protected from potential prying eyes by the solid balcony, he was naked, his skin hot, his cock starting to get hard as he ground against her. "Nice evening," he whispered.

"It would be if I'd been smart enough to bring a sweater."

"You came to Maine without a sweater? Bad girl!" Nick raised the T-shirt and gave her a few swats on the ass. "It gets cool here, even in summer." The whacks punctuating his "scolding" were light and playful, but, sensitive as her asscheeks were from earlier encounters with paddles, floggers, and her favorite hairbrush, they vibrated straight to her cunt. She pushed back, inviting more.

"Remember that first night, on your roof?" she purred.

"How could I forget? But while parts of me would love to relive that right now"—he rubbed his cock against her pussy lips to prove his point—"I'm starving."

Although the weekend's rules included "Nick sets the schedule," Eleanor was about to take a chance and protest, plead for a little more spanking and then his cock pushing into her from behind, pounding into her as the waves pounded the beach below.

Then she realized she too was borderline ravenous. Sure, they'd had a huge brunch and a late lunch, but between walking all over the picturesque village, playing in the surf, trying to outrun a thunderstorm, and having a lot of sex, they must have burned a million calories.

"Where are we going for dinner, sir? Should I dress up?"

"One of the lobster pounds. Got to keep it casual, since you'll be wearing one of my sweatshirts."

She giggled at the mental picture. Nick's sweatshirts were size extralarge and she was anything but.

Nick grabbed a handful of her hair, pulled her head back.

Her cunt clenched as he whispered in her ear, "Laugh now. You won't later."

Actually, she did laugh later, although it was more like nervous giggling, when they arrived at the restaurant with her in a little knit tank dress and Nick's gigantic, well-loved Northeastern sweatshirt.

She wasn't the only person in a makeshift outfit in the wake of the changed weather—about half the people in the restaurant were wearing cheap Ogunquit sweatshirts or fleeces with embroidered lobsters, obviously chosen in a hurry at one of the town's many gift shops, and several of the women were bundled into their male companions' sweaters or jackets.

But she was willing to bet she was the only one wearing a rope bra and corset under her clothes.

The only one so turned on she was worried about leaving telltale moisture on the chair.

The only one feeling that heady combination of confinement and freedom that bondage gave her, and the illicit thrill of knowing she was doing so in public. (Exhibitionism of the most discreet kind, since no one need ever know more than that she seemed happy, that her date seemed unusually attentive—and maybe that she'd thrown her back out or something, because she was sitting a little awkwardly, unable to lean back in her chair.)

The ropes Nick had used were soft, silky nylon, and they held her firmly without cutting. Whenever she drew a breath, she felt their embrace. The light pressure where they passed over her breastbone. The hug around her waist. The two strands that passed between her legs, tugging at her pussy lips.

Walking had been sweet torture, and Nick had insisted they walk from the hotel to the restaurant. Despite the foggy beauty of the evening, the scent of wild roses and ocean and rain-washed air along the coastal footpath called the Marginal Way, the constant sound of the waves on the rocks below, all she'd been able to think about were the sensations welling through her body.

By the time they made it to the restaurant, Nick was all but holding her up. Of course it hadn't helped that, in the guise of simple affection, he'd slipped his hand under the sweatshirt periodically to twist the knots that held everything together—constricting her waist, tightening the grip on her breasts so her nipples were almost painfully sensitive, separating her pussy lips, drenching her inner thighs.

Eleanor loved lobster with the passion of someone who'd grown up inland and knew it only as a special treat, but she ate in a daze, only vaguely aware of sweet, tender flesh bathed in warm butter, all too aware of her own tender flesh and the warm juices bathing them. Too aware of Nick eating with his hands in a deliberately sensual way—tearing into the lobster with a grin that suggested he was playing some kind of pleasure/pain game with it, licking his lips with every buttery bite, occasionally feeding her from his fingers even though they'd ordered the same meal.

Too aware that it would take his slightest touch to make her come.

Maybe not even a touch.

The right words, the right look would probably do it.

Her nipples throbbed with painful pleasure, so sensitive that the soft cotton knit of her dress brushing over them was sweet torture. It made her squirm in her seat, and that tugged at the ropes between her legs, tormenting her pussy lips, turning her clit into a hard, aching mass that made her imagine she knew what it felt like to have a cock.

When the waitress asked, "Would you like a look at the dessert menu?" Eleanor had to bite her tongue not to say no before Nick could answer. That, she knew, would count as topping from below and would have all but guaranteed she wouldn't get the orgasm she so badly needed, at least not until Nick had satisfied himself. Those were the rules they'd established for the weekend. They'd seemed reasonable at the time, but at the time, she hadn't been wrapped in rope and aching need.

To her relief, Nick asked for the check.

If the walk to the restaurant was a pleasant erotic torment, the walk back—each step tugging at her pussy lips, jouncing her over-sensitive breasts—was near-hell, painful in its intensity. Eleanor was crazy with arousal, her juices dripping down her thighs and soaking the ropes. Each step brought her more discomfort, but only because it brought her incrementally closer to the orgasm she couldn't quite reach. Nick, his arm around her, kept toying with the ropes or sliding his hand down to caress her bottom, adding to her pleasure and distress.

And since, despite the light mist, the Marginal Way was awash with tourists taking after-dinner strolls, Eleanor had to pretend she wasn't ready to crawl out of her skin with want, wasn't tempted to drag Nick to one of the benches overlooking the ocean and beg him to fuck her senseless.

By the time they turned off the Marginal Way onto the side path that led to the Beachmere, she was biting her lip to keep from sobbing—or screaming in a combination of lust and frustration.

Nick knew it. Once they were on that darker, quieter path, he tangled one hand in her hair and used the other to twist the ropes tighter, so tight that for a second her breath caught. "Come for me," he ordered.

And she did, stifling a scream against his shoulder, grinding her hips as if she were fucking the air.

"Good girl," he whispered. "That's my good girl."

Getting the rest of the way back to the Beachmere was easy enough—she floated on a cloud of endorphins and desire.

Floated through the lobby, down the hall. Up in the elevator to the third floor of the tower, into the darkened room.

Nick didn't turn on the lights. He just grabbed her, pulled her into a kiss that was both demanding and tender, a kiss that all but lifted her off the ground with its force.

"Please," she whimpered when he released her mouth, putting everything she wanted to say into that one fierce word, filling it with her want, her desire, her submission to him, the knowledge that whatever would happen next would happen on Nick's terms, not hers.

And the feeling she wasn't ready to put into words yet, even if she was capable of articulating, of something growing beyond the lust and the laughter and the craving for his body and his dominance.

It wasn't just that she'd never before known someone who'd think of this kind of exquisite erotic game.

It was more that if she had, she wouldn't have gone along with it. Not until Nick. Being out in public in that aroused, vulnerable state— a state of raw need, her body one exposed nerve—should have been frightening, as strange and disorienting as dining out stark naked. But instead, she realized, she'd felt safe because Nick was with her.

Something must have shown in her face, because Nick's voice dropped. In a ragged whisper, he said, "You're glowing. So beautiful. And see what you've done to me, just knowing you were wearing my ropes all this time."

He put one of her hands against his crotch so she could feel his hardness throbbing, waiting none too patiently for her.

She stroked him through his khakis, felt him twitch.

He seized her wrist, just roughly enough to remind her he was in charge. "Not here. On the balcony. Like our first night."

Mist still filled the air, but a full moon was peeping through the clouds, making a silvery trail over the ocean, leading onto the white sand of the distant beach. The ocean was still agitated from the afternoon's storm, and waves were breaking onto the rocks at the base of the Marginal Way. The air smelled salty and green, hinting of the lavender and roses and alyssum in the garden three stories below.

For a second, Eleanor leaned against the balcony, lost in a beauty strong enough that she almost forget why she was there, almost forgot the ropes under the clothes, her taut nipples, and her aching cunt.

Then Nick was behind her, pushing up her dress, sliding his cock between her hot, slick lips, between the ropes that separated and tormented them. The ocean spun away, and there was nothing in the world besides Nick, Nick's cock, her own burning need. Her fingernails dug into the painted wood of the balcony. She spread her legs further; leaned forward so her breasts, held together by coils of soft rope, pressed against the railing.

Nick entered her. His hips pounded with a rhythm like the waves crashing below. His fingers twined in the rope around her waist, pulling her back and forth as he desired. Each thrust tugged at the ropes on her pussy lips, moved her clit. Each thrust seemed to hit some spot deep inside her—not her G-spot or her cervix, although they were both getting into the act, making their own contributions to the waves of sensation breaking over her, but somewhere deeper, more integral and at the same time less tangible. Her soul, maybe, or her heart.

From the footpath below came the sound of laughter, voices. Nick whispered, "If they look up, they'll see us. They won't be able to see my cock in your pussy, but they'll be able to guess what we're doing. That you're riding my cock out here on the balcony like a slut." Then his voice caught, broke, and she could tell he was getting close. "My slut. My little tied-up bondage slut. Mine and no one else's."

His hips sped up, crashing into her, pushing her over the edge, shattering what little illusion of control she still harbored. Every muscle in her body tightened, and the ropes bit into her, and her cunt danced around Nick's cock as she cried out into the night.

And that did it for Nick. "Mine," he repeated. "Mine...always."

On the *always*, his body became abruptly still except for his cock, twitching inside her. Whether it was the twitching or the thought of being his always that set her off again she neither knew, nor, at that second, cared.

But she asked herself that much later.

After the ropes were long gone, after they'd cuddled and showered and made love again, a slower, more leisurely session with no bondage, no kink, just two tired, contented people enjoying the pleasure of touching each other; after Nick had dropped off to sleep, Eleanor lay in the dark asking herself what it meant. Had Nick meant "always" as in…well, always, or had it been one of those crazy things that pop out of your mouth when you're too busy coming to think?

And had her echo of, "Yours, always," been from the heart or just from the cunt?

She knew what her cunt's opinion was, had been since the first time Nick kissed her. "Yeah, baby! Keep this one!"

But was it good or dangerous that her heart was starting to agree?

NIKKI MAGENNIS

ESSENCE

VERYWHERE HE LOOKED, he thought he saw her. A certain image would catch his attention—a shadowed face, black hair splashing over a shoulder, delicate hands. He'd spot her on a street corner, in the canteen at university, on the TV screen, and his heart would leap. Then a stranger's face would turn to him and he'd feel the thud of loss. The hollow disappointment surprised him every time. His hopes exhausted him.

Only in the dry, rarified atmosphere of the lecture hall would he relax, knowing she would never follow him there. He stood at the lectern, hovering over the projector, watching his students as they sketched diagrams of flowers. One of his second-year students would suck her pencil as she listened to him recite the Latin names. When she raised her hand to answer a question, she spoke with a velvet voice.

"Sepal," she said. Edmond cleared his throat, smiled at her.

"Pollination, sir."

"Membrane." She winked at him.

Edmond marked her essays with red pen, lingering as he looked over the generous loops of her handwriting.

A+. Good work, Sophie!

In his overheated apartment, Edmond slept on a pillow stuffed with lavender. The soft reek of it was like antiseptic in his nose, but failed to erase the faint, faint smell that haunted his dreams.

Sometimes late at work in the lab, leaning over a microscope, he'd curl his upper lip and swear it was there, that scent, the smell that made his heart twist.

"Time to move on, Ed. Forget it," his friend Peter said as they sat in O'Neill's for a liquid lunch. Edmond nodded, dipped his head into his drink, and tried very hard not to think of how she had looked when they first met.

"Isn't Sophie enough to take your mind off it?"

Ah yes, there was Sophie. The eight-thirty date he'd almost forgotten—an evening of staring listlessly at those pneumatic bosoms over an expensive meal. Sophie with the perfect smile—hopeful, heart-stoppingly red, toothy and full.

That night, while he waited at the restaurant table with the city lights spread out beneath the balcony, Edmond let his mind drift across continents, across oceans. He pictured the fertile plains of manioc and grasses, and let his inner eye sweep over them, further. To the dark, swampy forest.

In the Wild

He followed her along a narrow path like a green tunnel, vines brushing against his face, mosquitoes whining past. All the time, he kept his eyes fixed on her, her lithe and narrow frame. Sweat soaked and breathless as he was fighting through the undergrowth, she was cool and quiet. She slid through the forest with ease, her long limbs moving like those of a creature who was perfectly at home, never seeming to feel the need to pause, always just ahead of him. Out of reach. She wasn't what most people would call beautiful—a downcast face, pale flesh, shadowed eyes that slid away from his every time he tried to lock his gaze on hers. Modest. He felt he was chasing some sprite of the forest, some hidden treasure. Moving onward, deeper into the forest, he followed her.

Under the table, Sophie was digging her stockinged foot into his crotch. Edmond shifted uneasily.

"What are your plans for the weekend?" she said. Actually, she lisped. The sound of her coy little-girl voice grated on Edmond's ear, just as her toes rubbed clumsily against his cock. He felt himself stiffen.

"Uh, I'm going to…"

"Yes?" Sophie corkscrewed her big toe against his balls. Her big sky-blue eyes went round.

"The Botanics."

"Tomorrow, right?" Sophie narrowed her eyes and licked her lips, her tongue flickering over the red lip-gloss. "But tonight you're going to take me home and fuck me senseless."

"Yes."

"Yes," she nodded. She scraped a spoonful of ice cream from her bowl, lifted it. "I'm looking forward to it, sir," she said, and winked as she slid the spoon into her mouth.

On the way home he kissed her and the powdered-sugar taste of her lips was almost enough.

Cultivation

Over the campfire, he watched her. The heat haze made the air flicker between them. Sparks popped and shot off into the darkness, the only noise apart from the crickets and night insects. Edmond drank his black tea, and thought hard. In his hot, damp, fevered brain, he searched for the word that would unlock her smile, the method that would bring her gently into his arms. More than he'd ever wanted anything, he wanted to be close to her. He was bewitched. Finally, he knew what had brought him there, what he'd been searching for all this time. They could melt into the black night together. He picked his moment carefully. When she leaned forward, he put out his hand and caught her. Held her gently, like a butterfly whose wings would flutter against the cage of his hands.

Back in his flat, they sat on the white leather couch and listened to a CD of Andean pipe music while Sophie French-kissed him. When she excused herself to go "take a tinkle," Edmond watched her curvaceous ass swing off toward the bathroom. He waited a moment and then pulled her purse toward him. Quickly, absentmindedly, he flipped it open and went through it. Credit cards, lipstick, cell phone. Two condoms like little brightly wrapped gifts. A mirror, in a plastic heart-shaped case. He removed his hand and smelt her strong, sickly perfume.

Sweating

It had taken longer than he could have imagined. Weeks of waiting, months of observation, a year of gentle persuasion to prepare the ground. It was something that couldn't be rushed—a rhythm that bowed to the movement of sun and wind as much as his desire and raging hormones. While he waited, all thoughts of his work and studies were forgotten. The humidity of the place soaked into his bones, turned him languid and unusually affable. He gave up counting, gave up taking notes and numbering specimens. Eventually, he lost all impatience and was content to watch the light play over her shy face. He'd sit with her in silence, a novel in his lap. Sometimes he'd read out a passage and see her nod in reply, perhaps understanding something in the tone of his voice if not the words he used. He'd toy with her hair, wind a tendril round his finger and tug softly. Teasing her.

At last, after months of careful attention, she was ready.

Sophie squeezed her breasts together and rubbed them in his face, against his silver stubble. He was smothered, coddled, surrounded by tit and swollen nipple. He sucked one into his mouth and she gasped. His hand went automatically to her cunt, which was shaved bare and smooth. He slid in two fingers, felt them swallowed in her hot grasp. Inside that flesh, such slippery ease, his knuckles felt thick and arthritic. She spread her legs wider. He pushed her clit with the one-two action that he knew would arouse her. She jerked back and cried out. Then she rolled over and sat on him, running the wet lips of her cunt up and down him like a pole dancer, working hard. Finally, she stuck herself on top of him, skewered herself on his cock and bounced, her big perky tits quaking beautifully as she moved up and down.

"Come on, baby. Fuck me good."

His cock slipped in and out, hit the G-spot bang on target. He felt his sperm boosting up inside him and his balls tighten. With a moan, he let it go, a small and neat explosion into the rubber teat.

Sophie cried extravagantly when she came, a kitten meowing against his shoulder. They waited ten minutes, then started again.

Afterward, he lay awake watching the dawn bleach the sky. Sophie's arm was locked around his waist, her hand a fist, the long nails perfectly polished and traces of his dried semen between her fingers. As she slept, her face at last seemed soft enough to remember.

They lay together on the forest floor with the night surrounding them, and she made only the faintest noise as he put his hand there, as he opened her lips delicately. Inside she was sticky, and when he bent his face down to taste her she was sweet. What he remembered the most, though, was the smell. Tobacco, licorice. Something he couldn't describe, familiar but elusive. She was smoky and pungent and delicious and he could suck at her like a bee drinking nectar.

Synthesis

The Botanics were crowded, full of Saturday afternoon visitors: families, crying children, a sloppily dressed teenager who looked stoned out of his head. Gardeners in green overalls raked gravel and pulled away dead leaves. Edmond nodded to a couple of the older guys as he passed. He bent to look at the tag on a date palm, made a mental note. Sophie walked swiftly round the Temperate section, blowing air up into her bangs.

"Jesus, it's hot in here. What was it you wanted to see?"

Her voice was loud and flat against the glasshouse walls, and Edmond noticed her makeup clogging on her face. The humidity soaked into his skin, misted his hair with fine droplets.

He couldn't stop himself; he looked down at her long, naked legs. Hot? In that tiny skirt? Then he saw the glimmer hazed over her flesh, realized she was wearing nylons.

"Edmond? You done yet?" She looked at him as he lingered in front of the doorway that led to the Tropical House. There, it was there. The smell that he'd been searching for. Sophie's eau de parfum nearly overpowered it, but it was there nonetheless. A smoky, elusive scent. A dark and tantalizing smell that grew stronger as he walked toward the doorway.

"How about we get out of here?" Sophie was right beside him, clutching at his arm. She leaned in close to his ear and whispered, her breath making his neck itch. "I'm horny. Let's go back to your place."

"No," Edmond said. "No, I don't think so." He turned one last time to look at her. "I'm sorry, Sophie."

"I *fuck* your pardon?" said Sophie, her crimson lips drawing back over her teeth and her eyes cracking in confusion. "You're turning me down? Who the hell... Now, hold on one minute, mister—are you married?"

The noise of the sprinklers roared into the space between them, spraying a false mist into the hothouse air. Sophie gave a harsh, short bark of a laugh.

"Oh yeah? Well, Christ, you're not doing badly for an old pervert, are you *sir*?" With that, she spun on her heel, marched off toward the green EXIT sign.

And Edmond walked to the doorway, stepped into the green and moist room and let his lungs fill with the scent. She was here, she'd always been here. He'd brought her halfway round the world and then had to leave her. She'd have sickened in his cold, dry life, and the lonely luxury of his sparse flat downtown. She needed the damp earth and the heat of the tropics, needed familiar surroundings, even if they were contained inside a huge glass cage. He hadn't been able to take her with him, yet he couldn't ever really leave her behind.

Sophie, the other women, they were cheap imitations. They never came close. Fake tits, fake smiles, fake orgasms. Blowsy and bright and beautiful, they were eye-catching temptations that quickly turned sour.

He turned a corner. Here she was. In the shadows she waited silently, hung with virgin flowers. Waiting for him to pull her apart, to kiss her together again. To dip his tongue into her dark crevices and make her sweat. He would stay with her this time, in silence and awe, waiting for the one night a year when she would open to him.

Vanilla. He could taste her on his lips. Everywhere.

ALISON TYLER

UN, DEUX, TROIS

EUROPE TRANSFORMS ME.

I've been nearly a dozen times over the years, and on each trip, a magical change takes place almost as soon as I step off the plane. I wear clothes abroad that I'd never wear at home. I buy shoes that would seem ridiculous in my daily life. I exude confidence like you wouldn't believe.

But being with Jack in Paris was something else.

"Where are we?" I asked, shifting nervously from one foot to the other.

"Paris," Jack replied smugly.

"But where…"

"Sh, baby. Just wait. You'll see…."

The two of us stood outside of a nondescript stone building. Jack was exquisitely dressed, in black, of course. The man knew how to wear black. Fine slacks. Long-sleeved shirt under a V-neck sweater. The only color coming from the glow in his dark blue eyes.

He'd dressed me, as well, in the most exquisite ebony cocktail dress. White collar and cuffs. Obsidian buttons running from neck to hem. Hose to match and stacked patent-leather pumps. My nerves completed the outfit. Shivery and shimmery—chaos running through my body.

A small window slid open in the door and I realized that someone was watching us, but I couldn't see whether the person was male or female, young or old. Jack stepped close, said something in French, then spelled his last name, and the window closed. In seconds, the door was opened for us, and we were allowed to enter.

I blinked rapidly, trying to grow acclimated to the poorly lit surroundings. Jack followed after the person who'd opened the door for us, but he blocked my view in the narrow passageway. I guessed that the person was female by the click-clack of heels on stone floor, yet I couldn't see for sure.

Candles flickered, creating golden halos of light. And then we were at the end of the hall, and into a main room, where a rippling black ceiling looked as if it were made of roiling water. Jack pulled me by my wrist after him, settling us on a love seat against the far wall. A hostess approached immediately wearing the shortest of dresses, a tiny black number that clung to her sleek figure. She gave Jack an appraising nod, then looked at me and smirked. I must have appeared like a gawky teen, staring at everything at once, trying to make sense of the place.

It might simply have been a disco. There was a bar in one corner. A glittery disco ball in the center of the sensuous black ceiling. Mirrors on the walls. But there was also a mammoth canopy bed in the center of the room. Everywhere I looked, I saw beautiful couples. Women dressed elegantly. Men in suits or slightly more casual attire, like Jack's. Many were dancing. Some were sitting on sofas or love seats, drinking from champagne flutes.

While I stared, the waitress left and returned with two glasses of champagne. I sipped from my glass, and continued to observe my surroundings. Jack hadn't taken me here to dance. I was sure of that. But he'd given me no clue as to why we *were* here. And then slowly, I started to get a picture.

Across the room was a large group, three couples, the men slightly older than the women, perhaps in their fifties, while the women were early forties and very chic. While I watched, one of these women stood up to dance for her companions. Sensuously, her hips rolling like the waves in the ceiling, she undid her dress and let it fall away. In moments, she was down to a black bra and panty set, her heels, and her long blonde hair. And she was reflected in the mirrors on the wall, a goddess, a vision, so striking in a sea of black.

Jack watched her, and then watched me watch her. And then, as if on cue, several other women nearby began to shed their clothes. One after another. A rippling effect. The hostesses were there to scoop up the belongings, to hang them on hooks behind the bar. But the vision was mesmerizing.

The men dressed. The women stripping down.

So elegantly. So slowly.

Jack's hand rested on my knee. He leaned in close and gave me another kiss, and then he led me onto the dance floor and under the mirrored ball.

Some of the women still had their street clothes on, but most were down to the most delicate, dainty underthings. Paris is definitely the lingerie capital, and these women—all French, apparently, from the snippets of conversation I could make out—were doing their part to advertise the finery of their city.

Jack didn't seem to be paying any notice. He danced with me, protecting me with his body when people moved too close, keeping me precisely where he wanted me. The music was surprising. I'd have expected a heavy techno beat. But what we got was pure rock. Aerosmith. The Stones. Robert Palmer. T. Rex.

Suddenly, the lights in the room, already dim, seemed to dip even lower, and I felt a noticeable change. Jack had his hand on me, tightly gripping my shoulder, and he moved me back to the crimson love seat where we'd started.

Was the room emptying?

Had people left?

I looked at Jack, waiting for him to explain, but he didn't say a word. Now, I tried to pay more careful attention. Glancing around the room, I realized that the group of six, with the sultry blonde who had led the impromptu stripping, had disappeared. So had a few of the other couples I'd been watching. Then finally I saw that couples, or groups of couples, were heading down a corridor, turning around a corner and disappearing.

Jack had his arm around my shoulder. He seemed fine with staying exactly where we were, sipping fresh glasses of champagne and watching the last few couples on the dance floor. Now, every girl out there was down to some form of underclothes. Camisole and tap panties. Thong and demi-cup bra. A range of items in a rainbow of colors. The men were all fully dressed, which added a further element of intrigue to the situation: what was going to happen next?

When I gazed around again, I realized I was one of only a handful of girls who still had clothes on. But Jack wasn't pushing me. Wasn't saying anything at all. He seemed content to be an observer, watching for once, an audience member rather than a player.

My mind was so filled with queries, I missed another important segue. The one in which two couples made the first plunge onto the mattress. One was the sultry blonde and her older partner. They'd returned from wherever their adventure had taken them, and now, the man seemed intent on matching the woman's exhibitionist streak. I sucked in my breath as he slid her panties down her long, lean legs; as he bent down between them and began to lick her. Another couple from their party was close by, helping. Removing the woman's bra. Stroking her hair out of her face.

She was the star right now, and we all watched. Wet as she became wet.

Breathless, as she became breathless.

The blonde on the bed seemed to swoon in pleasure. Her long hair was beautifully arranged on the pillow, spread around her head like ribbons of gold. The sheets on the bed were satin, and black like the roiling ceiling; black water, churning under her pale skin.

Her body was made to be adored, tight muscles, flat stomach, and those long, lean legs. She still had on her heels, which made her look extra sexy. As if she couldn't be bothered to take off her pumps. That's what I thought at first, but then a man came forward to the foot of the bed, and he bent and cradled one of her feet in his hands and began to slowly tongue the leather of the shoe. My heart pounded.

A hostess brought me a fresh glass of champagne and I looked over at Jack, surprised, but he only winked. Had he ordered more? I hadn't noticed. There were too many things for me to focus on at once. The music continued in the throbbing, sexy vein. Prince, now. A low rumble. A sultry groove.

Couples had taken all of the love seats, making out as if we were in somebody's parents' high-end rec room. Limbs overlapping. Nestled together. But when I looked at the center of the room, I saw that there were more people on the bed now. Were they all from the blonde's original party? Or had strangers joined in? Things were happening too fast for me. Or maybe it was the champagne. I had that waking dream feeling—a sensation I got with Jack quite often—my eyes unable to take in everything that was going on at once.

Because right next to us, on the couch to our left, a woman was giving her boyfriend a hand job. When had that happened? When had she gone on her knees next to him, and undone his black slacks?

Her hand job progressed naturally to a blow job, her mouth open and hungry, drawing in her partner's cock.

Jack seemed charmed by my wide eyes.

"You like?" he asked softly

I nodded.

"Are you ready?"

And now I paid attention. Jack was giving me a clue, getting me set.

"For what, Jack?"

"For the next level."

Like a video game. You make it to the higher level if you pass through the challenges on the first. But unlike in a video game, in which you progress upward, Jack took me by the hand, walked me across the club, and led me down....

The club seemed to be carved from stone. As we made our way down a spiral staircase, I immediately recalled a previous trip to Paris. A visit to the famous catacombs. The air grew colder with each step we took, and Jack tightened his grip on me, making sure I didn't slip in my heels.

The staircase was tight and narrow, and I felt as if we were journeying underwater. A chill ran through me until we reached level number two. There were beds here. In every nook. Every corner. Satin-sheeted mattresses. Lounges in velvet. In fact, there was hardly any floor space not taken over by some sort of area in which to fuck.

And people *were* fucking.

Jack let me press back against him, so that we were as flat against one wall as we could be, and I could feel how hard he was through his slacks. I experienced a wave of gratefulness that he had not made me strip upstairs. That he had not positioned me on one of these beds. But I also felt lust flow through me. The players were beautiful. That was the common denominator. Some older, some my age, but all so elegant. Well-coiffed hair. Gym-hard bodies.

Even with all the fucking going on around us, there was nothing seedy about the place. How was that possible? I didn't know. I just watched. Listened. Heard the moans and sighs. Noticed when the voyeurs would shift their attention from one sofa to another. You could almost chart the sexual energy in the room. As one group reached a fever pitch, others hurried to witness the explosions. And then, of course, another bang would go off like firecrackers in a different part of the room, and all would rush over to see. To be part of the excitement, if only vicariously.

"What do you think?" Jack murmured, hands around me, holding me tight.

I didn't have words to tell him. I would have stood there, jaw open, eyes wide, for hours. This was like nothing I'd ever seen before. Because in so many ways, it didn't feel real.

"Answer me."

I turned to look at him over my shoulder.... What was he asking? Did he truly want to know how hard my heart was pounding? Or was he trying to determine whether or not I was ready to join in? To dive in amongst the sensuous, writhing bodies. To find my own place on a mattress in a corner. Nobody else was talking. Everyone seemed as hypnotized, as mesmerized, as I felt.

"I don't know what to think."

"But you like it?"

"Yes, Jack."

"Who do you like best?"

I scanned the closest beds, the nearest lounges. There were so many pretty connections taking place near to us. Two gorgeous girls working the same man. Two men helping themselves to the parted thighs of one young redhead.

"Them," I finally said, locating one of my more pedestrian fantasies. The men were slightly older than their female partners. One had his girl in front of him, and was pulling on her hair as he fucked her.

"Yes," Jack sighed. "That's nice, isn't it?" As if he were commenting on a sip of good wine. Nice.

But the one thing I realized as I looked around the room was that nothing actually kinky was occurring. There were no bindings. No blindfolds. No cuffs. Just sex. Overlapping bodies. More than ménages. So that when Jack undid his slacks and pushed me forward, when he found a space for us on the nearest vacated sofa and lifted my skirt, when his hand came down automatically on my ass, the crack of the sound brought all eyes to us. Drew a crowd around us, right from the start....

Jack didn't spank me in any "normal" way. He didn't pull my panties down slowly, to make me feel truly exposed. His hand met my ass because... That's the only reason: because. The sound of the connection, the response I gave him. This was straight sex for us. Vanilla sex. With me in front of him bent over, and him behind. We were both still fully dressed, which made us an aberration from the start. But it was the fact that he was spanking me that drew the people in.

I kept my head down, arms locked, eyes closed, trying to get through the feeling of being on display. Trying to tell myself that we were simply one more couple in a very busy couples' club.

The voyeurs came closer when we began fucking. They seemed drawn to us. And in moments I felt hands on me. Tentatively at first. Fingers slipping over my face, pushing my bangs out of my eyes. Then hands on my arms, and interlacing my fingers. And I couldn't help myself any longer. I had to open my eyes. I had to see what was going on. If I kept my eyes closed, I could pretend that Jack and I were by ourselves. But once I opened my eyes, once I committed to the situation, my heart began to pound. There were couples close by. Truly close, so that their heat became my heat.

People spoke to me. Spoke to Jack. And he responded, although I couldn't. They were all talking in French. Whispering to us. Praising us, I would guess, from the expressions on their faces. Jack could answer. Every so often, he'd respond. But I was lost in my world, not fathoming a word.

Jack kept up the rhythm, fucking me hard, letting me know how turned on he was by the speed with which he took me. There was no going slow right now. No lingering. Jack put both of his hands on my waist, pulling me back into him, and he came.

I could see that another couple—no, a foursome—nearby was drawing away part of our crowd. Ricocheting fireworks, like I'd thought before. But many of the group stayed close by, as if wanting an encore. Or hoping for something else. Something different. We'd surprised them. That was clear. I could tell from the hungry look on the audience's faces that we had given them only a mere taste of what they hoped for.

And Jack, like any good ringmaster, wasn't going to disappoint. I glanced over my shoulder at him when I heard the sound of his belt being pulled free.

"Tuck up your dress," he said, but before I could, some helpful hands did the deed for me, pulling the hem of my dress high up to my waist. I felt something inside of me snap. The fear faded, leaving only lust in its place.

My panties were down, but not off, and Jack waited for a blonde near my side to pull them over my heels. Had he said something to her, or did she just know? The people nearby moved back a little, to give Jack space—even in a place where space was the one commodity not readily available.

"Ten," Jack said, and I felt myself attempt to get ready. Muscles tightening automatically, and then slowly starting to relax as he made me wait.

A girl moved closer to me, so close that she and I were face-to-face. She cradled my face in her hands, and I knew she could see Jack over my head. She knew when he was going to strike, and she kissed me at that very moment. Kissed me sweetly, softly, so that pain met pleasure in one brutal moment.

Ten. Ten's nothing. Ten's cake. Or icing.

If Jack had told me to count out ten in the privacy of the hotel, or back at home, or even in a car, the concept would have been laughable. A game of pat-a-cake that Jack never would have thought to engage in. Ten wouldn't even have counted as foreplay in our world.

But ten strokes of Jack's belt in public, with a stunning stranger touching my face, kissing my lips...that was different. That was intense. Enlightening, even. We were in this underground world filled with the turbulent motion of sex and bodies. Moving to the erotic soundtrack of moans and sighs. Witnesses to the bliss of nearby players, their sounds echoing, reverberating around us.

And then there was Jack and his belt.

Punishing me, or pleasuring me?

The answer to that depends entirely on how you look at what Jack and I did together. For me, of course, the definition was one and the same.

I counted, slowly, softly, and the girl counted with me in French:

One—*un*.

Two—*deux*.

Three—*trois*.

Giving me ten kisses for the ten strokes. Her lips were heavenly soft but she didn't try to increase the passion between us. She gave me sweet, chaste kisses on the lips each time Jack landed a blow on my naked skin. And somehow that made everything even more surreal than it already felt. If she'd gripped me tightly, if she'd touched me with possession, that would have been almost expected. Another Dom in our midst. But her fingertips were as light as her lips, and she seemed content to simply coexist with me, partake of the blows as more than a witness but less than a participant.

How had she found us?

Had she been watching us? Had she seen us on the dance floor, or cuddled on the sofa? Or had she simply been drawn over when Jack first let his hand smack against my ass? That sound a striking call to all submissive souls.

Come. Join us. Seek out what you crave.

I tried my best to stay focused in the moment, tried to pay attention to the girl's heart-shaped face, to the candy taste of her lips, to the way her caramel-colored hair fell into her blue eyes. We reached ten. Ten smarting blows on my upturned ass, before Jack slid his belt back into place. There seemed to be a collective sigh around us, as if people were sad that the show was over. I wondered if it really was. If the curtain had come down on us. Or if Jack was simply preparing for the next step.

I felt his hands on me, pulling my dress back into place, grabbing up my panties. The girl sat down on her haunches, watching warily. More feline than she'd seemed before. Showing off power that I hadn't recognized at first. She didn't seem to like the fact that Jack was moving me away from her, standing between us. Jack didn't pay her the slightest bit of attention.

He gathered me up in his arms, blocking out the crowd. From the look on his face, he didn't seem disturbed that I'd kissed the girl—or been kissed by her—but he also seemed finished with the exhibition. Jack had me in motion, hustling me back up the stairs, telling the hostesses we were ready for our coats—I made out those words—and then handing over money.

Then we were out, into the night, walking through the darkened streets of Paris. Walking hand in hand, as if we were a normal couple. Lovers out for a midnight stroll.

Yes, Europe transforms me.

But not as much as Jack does.

ABOUT THE EDITOR

C ALLED "A TROLLOP WITH A LAPTOP" by *East Bay Express*, and a "literary siren" by Good Vibrations, Alison Tyler is naughty and she knows it. Ms. Tyler is the author of more than twenty explicit novels, including *Learning to Love It*, *Strictly Confidential*, *Sweet Thing*, *Sticky Fingers*, *Something About Workmen*, *Rumors*, *Tiffany Twisted* and *With or Without You* (Cheek). Her short stories have appeared in more than seventy anthologies and have been translated into Spanish, German, Italian, Japanese, Greek and Dutch.

She is the editor of thirty-five anthologies including *Heat Wave*, *Best Bondage Erotica* volumes 1 & 2, *The Merry XXXMas Book of Erotica*, *Luscious*, *Red Hot Erotica*, *Slave to Love*, *Three-Way*, *Happy Birthday Erotica* (all from Cleis Press); *Naughty Fairy Tales from A to Z* (Plume); and the *Naughty Stories from A to Z* series, the *Down & Dirty* series, *Naked Erotica* and *Juicy Erotica* (all from Pretty Things Press). Please visit www.prettythingspress.com.

Ms. Tyler is loyal to coffee (black), lipstick (red), and tequila (straight). She has tattoos, but no piercings; a wicked tongue, but a quick smile; and bittersweet memories, but no regrets. She believes it won't rain if she doesn't bring an umbrella, prefers hot and dry to cold and wet, and loves to spout her favorite motto: "You can sleep when you're dead." She chooses Led Zeppelin over the Beatles, the Cure over the Smiths, and the Stones over everyone—yet although she appreciates good rock, she has a pitiful weakness for '80s hair bands.

In all things important, she remains faithful to her partner of over a decade, but she still can't choose just one perfume.